Saving Superman

Book 1

Saving Superman Saga

Kathleen Sales

Saving Superman

2nd Edition

This is a work of fiction. All of the characters, names, incidents, organizations, and dialogue in this novel are either the products of the author's imagination or are used fictitiously.

Library of Congress Control Number: 2013919344

ISBN: 978-1-7352361-0-0 (sc)
ISBN: 978-1-7352361-1-7 (e)

Cover by Al Esper

Dedication

I dedicate *Saving Superman* to Neil Dye.

Without his understanding and compassion, none of
my stories would ever have been told,
much less written.

Acknowledgements

Thanks to the wonderful classes taught by Steve Alcorn, writing the first draft of *Saving Superman* was easy, but getting it ready for publication required many helping hands. I would like to thank my readers, Joyce Leo and Brian Sales.

My editor, Cathy Kodra, deserves much praise as she patiently walked me through the rules of modern grammar while offering excellent rewrite suggestions. Other editors of note include Nancy Johansen who read the novel and provided several pages of constructive criticism.

Al Esper created the beautiful new cover and was a joy to work with.

Thank you all!

Chapter 1

On a muggy August morning in 1956, I ran away. Two days down the road, footsore and hungry, I kept walking because I had nowhere else to go. I'd just reached a crossroads when an ear-splitting thunderclap stopped me in my tracks, and before I could recover, the heavens opened up and drowned me. I turned, running straight into the storm. My feet slapped hard and fast on the flooded asphalt, my head tilted back so I could drink. The lightning and thunder cracked all around, and maybe I was crazy, but right then I felt like Superman.

Another mile down the road, the rain eased. In front of me lay huge mounds of trash, ragged garments, broken chairs, and soggy garbage bags leaking their innards into puddles on the ground. I began exploring, hoping to find food or a canteen. But as I rummaged through the piles, the thunderclouds grew black, and shifting winds swirled the trash into mini-cyclones. I postponed my hunt and searched for shelter.

On a ridge past the dump, I spied what looked to be small buildings. I climbed the slope. Stacks of plywood topped with metal sheets rose above me. Concrete block and bricks stood further back. And right behind them, I saw a shed. Built only from metal sheets tied to a frame, it wouldn't protect me from a dangerous storm. But it would be drier, and with that thought in mind, I approached.

A huge bear reared up in the doorway. I jumped back. But then I saw the ragged clothes and realized it was human, probably a hobo or a bum. His shaggy hair and beard were brown streaked with gray, and as he looked down at me, I saw gaps between his teeth and bright blue eyes sunk deep beneath his brows. We stared at each other without speaking 'til he growled, "Well boy, what you want?"

My heart thumped in my chest. Was he dangerous? Would he hurt me? Did he have a gun inside that shed? And while I was struggling to decide, the storm hit. The shed shook and rattled in the sudden gusts of wind, its metal roof straining to break free. But as I backed away, the black sky pelted me with hail. I threw my arms across my face while icy bullets battered and bounced off my back, quickly melting to ice water in my shoes.

I started shivering so hard I couldn't stand it, and my feet inched closer to the door. "Please, can I come in? Just 'til it stops?"

The man grunted. I wasn't sure whether that meant yes or no, but then he moved and let me step inside. I stood trembling as rainwater streamed off my clothes and formed into puddles on the plywood. He frowned and grabbed a sleeping bag. "Take off your clothes and climb in here."

At any other time I would have fled, but I was weak from running, soaked to the skin, and shivering so hard my teeth began to rattle. I peeled off my sneakers, shirt, and jeans and climbed inside the sleeping bag to strip completely bare. When the man moved toward me, I grabbed the bag real tight. He just took my clothes, wrung them hard outside the shed, and spread them on a tabletop to dry.

Trapped like a caterpillar inside its cocoon, I peered out at my dimly lit surroundings. The man stayed near the door, staring out into the rain. Behind him stood a bed built from orange crates and a mattress. The table with my clothes sat opposite the bed and rested on a base made from crisscrossed two by fours. Next to my clothes, I saw a lantern and some kitchenware. And when I turned around, I glimpsed a bookcase behind me, its sagging shelves lined with cans of food.

The hail beat a deafening drum roll on the roof. Then it stopped, and I heard the steady sound of pouring rain. I watched the man. He sat down on his bed and kept staring at the storm, at my clothes, and then at me. I was regretting my decision to come in when he spoke in a gravelly, bass voice.

"What's your name?"

"Pete."

"How old are you?"

"Eleven," I lied, but it'd be true within a year.

"You live nearby?"

I shook my head, unwilling to explain. I'd already spent more than two days on the road. The first night I'd slept beneath a haystack in a field, the second in a barn where I'd stolen several eggs. Today I hadn't eaten, but I was *not* ready to go back.

The man pursed his lips and stared at me, his brows pulled together in a thoughtful frown. I feared he'd get angry, and I couldn't run without my clothes. But after a bit, his face relaxed. I figured he'd judged me and decided on my fate, and like any prisoner, I waited on the verdict.

"Hungry?" he asked.

My eyes widened and my stomach growled.

"All I got here is canned beans. That okay?"

I nodded—any food sounded good to me. He spooned cold beans from the can onto a plate. I'd hoped he would warm them, but it didn't really matter as I shoveled down every bite. He emptied the remainder into a bowl and helped himself. Then he handed me a stale piece of bread—I ate that too.

"As soon as your clothes dry, I'll walk you home," he said. "Where do you live?"

I started to object, and he held up a massive hand. But cuddled warm and comfortable inside his sleeping bag, with his food in my belly, I didn't take that warning seriously. "No one's there," I explained.

"You an orphan?"

"No, sir. Ma's in the hospital and Pa's up in Kentucky where he works in the mine all week long." I hoped that'd be enough to give him pause, although I still expected him to push for my address.

Instead, he asked, "What's wrong with your ma?"

His question caught me totally off guard, and I stared at the floor to hide my face. He waited, munching slowly on his bread. When I couldn't find words to explain what she'd done, I simply told him, "She's too sad."

"Depressed?"

I couldn't answer as ugly memories flooded through my brain, images I didn't want to think, much less say.

The man frowned as he reached to check my clothes—still wet. But when he turned and saw me, his eyes opened in surprise, and he appeared more concerned than angry. He had good reason for concern: my heart raced in my chest, I struggled to breathe, and my brain felt so muddled, I couldn't even think. I feared losing control and prayed this nosy person would stop asking dangerous questions. But he didn't.

"Do you know why she's sad? Did someone die?"

Pressure built behind my eyes; I fought back tears. That death tore at my family like a dog tears a rabbit. Ma said it was my fault, but I had no idea what I'd done.

I started sobbing, and for several minutes the only sound inside that shed was me, bawling. The man said nothing, but he didn't try to hit me, or yell, or throw me out into the rain. I cried until all my tears were gone. Then I looked for a tissue, but that was a lost cause, so I blew my nose on his sleeping bag.

When I glanced up, the man was staring into space. Pa got that look from time to time, and if you messed with him, he'd crack you a hard lick. I waited. Eventually the man sighed and turned to look at me. His sharp blue eyes pierced my mind like needles, and I felt them peeking into my most secret fears. After the crying jag, I was defenseless, a helpless puppet in his hands.

"Well," he finally said. "Since your parents aren't at home, maybe you should tell me what's got you so upset."

I looked up and tried to read his face. The blue eyes softened, and his curious expression led me to believe he actually wanted me to tell him the whole truth. That wasn't my experience with adults. They usually had something in mind for you to say and refused to listen when you said something different. But this guy didn't fit that mold, and just for that reason, I started to tell him the whole story.

I paused, trying to organize my thoughts. The man sat quietly, giving me all the time I needed.

"He woulda been my baby brother," I began.

The man nodded, his eyes intent on me.

"It was early May, and I was home with a cold. I could hear Mamaw in the bedroom with Ma."

"Were they talking?"

"No. Ma was cryin' and screamin', and Mamaw yelled, 'Push hard!' Then Ma screamed even louder. But after that they got real quiet."

"The baby didn't cry?"

"That's why I snuck into the bathroom. Then I saw him, in the sink."

"Was he alive?"

I shrugged and frowned. "He was tiny, kinda blue, and streaked with blood."

I'd known immediately that something was bad wrong and wondered if maybe I could fix him. I would have slapped him on his fanny or done mouth-to-mouth breathing, but no one ever showed me how to do either one, and I was too afraid to try.

"Was anybody else there?"

"Mamaw. She found me."

"What'd she do?"

"She told me to go and get a shoebox from Pa's closet. And after I got back, she washed him clean."

He nodded. "What happened next?"

"She put him in the shoebox and told me I could touch him. But he felt cold and slimy—like a *fish!*"

"'Cause he was dead," the man explained, and the corners of his mouth and eyes drooped.

I stared at the floor, too miserable to talk. I'd wanted a brother. I wanted him to be the baby in the family so I could be the big brother for a change. And I couldn't stop thinking that I'd done something wrong and made my baby brother die.

"Was there anythin' I coulda done to save him?"

The man was silent for a moment. "Maybe, but once someone's dead, you can't change it. And your brother probably died while being born."

That idea made me feel a little better. But the weight of my guilt still hung over me, a rotten branch waiting for a squall.

"Did you bury him?" he asked.

"Yeah, after Pa got home."

I didn't feel like going into detail, but my mind saw it clear as yesterday. I helped Pa build a wooden box, and then he dug a deep hole under the old redbud tree out back. We all stood around it and sang hymns. Pa read from the Bible before he put the wooden box down inside the hole. But the worst part, at least for me, was shoveling back the dirt. I felt wicked for covering my brother up with dirt.

The man was quiet too. At his age, he'd probably seen a lot of funerals. When he spoke next, he surprised me. "Was your ma any happier before she lost the baby?"

"No!" I snapped. "She was either sad or mad, and mostly mad at me." I closed my mouth to stop my hateful words. Mamaw had explained that Ma was sick, and maybe she was right. In some distant memory, which felt more like a dream, I saw Ma laughing. She used to sing, read to me, and smile. I wanted that Ma back and couldn't figure out where she'd gone.

"She was a singer," I explained. "And durin' the war, she sang in Nashville. Lots of important people thought she'd become famous. But after Pa came home, Ma had me. So it's my fault she got stuck in Walnut Springs."

Oops! I'd told him where I lived. But he didn't change expression and continued to take seriously everything I said. It felt weird to have anyone pay such close attention. I liked it. Ma never talked with me, Mamaw was too busy, and nowadays Pa was never there.

I glanced up at the man, and his bearded face looked puzzled. Then he asked, "Do you have any brothers or sisters?"

"Just Sarah, she's almost four years older. Mamaw took care of her while Ma sang in Nashville. But Mamaw said I was one too many."

"And then your ma went and had another." The man shook his head as if that puzzle went beyond his understanding. He glanced outside. The rain had stopped, and the sun was peeking out from behind a towering black cloud. "I'm going for a walk. You can stay here if you want." And with that, he left the shed and disappeared. Since I was buck naked, I curled up in the sleeping bag and slept.

Chapter 2

When I woke, the sun was setting in the west, streaking the remaining clouds with shades of pink and red. I stood at the doorway and squinted in the glare. Past the piled stacks, I saw the man. He was gathering up metal sheets and plywood, which had blown from their stacks during the storm. I realized it was time for me to leave, or else he might come and drag me back to Walnut Springs. I put on my clothes, which were mostly dried, and forced my soggy sneakers on my feet. Then I checked my pocket for my *Superman* comic book and the little flag I used as a bookmark. They were there.

I was walking through the doorway when the man reappeared.

"You leaving?" he asked.

"Yeah. Thanks for lettin' me dry out, and everythin'." I felt more than a little bit embarrassed, remembering how I cried and told him all about my brother.

"Where you headed?"

I pointed toward the sunset. My general plan was to walk to Nashville, and if I made it, maybe farther west.

"You have family there?"

"Kinda."

He cocked his head and waited.

"Well, Aunt Kate, Ma's sister, lives outside of Nashville."

"Is she expecting you?"

I hung my head. He sighed and watched the sun as it dropped behind the mountains.

"It takes a week to walk to Nashville. I know; I hiked it once. Better to start out in the morning when it's light. If you want to sleep here, I can make you a pallet on the floor."

I hesitated, but then he put a paper bag down on the table. "I went shopping and bought us some fried chicken. At least fuel up before you go."

When he opened the bag, its aroma filled the air and made my decision much too easy. I sat down on the bed as he divided up the pieces on two plates and dished out coleslaw. I dug in. After we ate, he took the mattress off the orange crates and pulled a couple blankets out of their hiding place.

"I use these in winter, but it won't be that cold, so you'll only need the one tonight."

"Thanks." And I meant it. At home, we owned a closet full of blankets, so getting one wasn't a big deal. But this guy shared everything he had, even food, and that made it special, like a gift.

He spread the sleeping bag out on the floor, and I lay down. Then he threw a blanket over me. He grabbed the other blanket and stretched out on his bed. "By the way," he said, "since you're spending the night, I'd like to know your full name."

"Pete Martin."

"That's a good name." I could hear his smile. "I go by Jake."

He didn't mention his last name, and Mamaw always told me to use Mister with men. "Should I call you Mister Jake?"

He laughed, a deep belly laugh that shook the makeshift bed. "Now that's a hoot. No, just call me Jake. That'd be okay."

Did he have a last name? Why was he living in a shed? Where was he from? Too curious to keep still, I asked, "You live here long?"

"A couple years. A builder owns this land, and he stores a lot of his building supplies here. I make sure nobody steals them."

That made sense. "Where did you live before?"

"I rode the rails. And before that, I sailed and worked on ships. I've been all around the world, more than once, and up and down the west coast so often I've lost count."

"Wow!" Nashville seemed a long way off to me, but he'd probably been to South America or China. "Why stay here?"

Jake didn't answer for a bit. "Guess I'm getting old and tired, need a place to rest."

He sounded tired, so I stopped asking questions and started saying prayers. I prayed out loud, the same as we did at home. Jake listened in silence while I asked the Lord Jesus to forgive my sins and watch over all my family. I didn't hear Jake pray, but he might have said a silent prayer. Then he turned off the lantern, which he'd lit before our meal, and we lay there listening to the tree frogs and cicadas.

I must have nodded off, because I found myself curled up in a soft velvet chair, half-asleep, listening to music. Somewhere close beside me, people laughed, a man played jazz on the piano, and Ma sang. I loved the sound of her sweet voice. Then I heard screams, and strange men came running in, with *guns!* Ma shrieked…a huge man grabbed me by my hair…his gun pressed against my throat…*I screamed*…

"Easy there, Pete. You're safe. You're okay." Jake reached out with his hand and touched my arm. "It was just a dream; go back to sleep."

I tried, but I tossed and turned for hours. I couldn't sleep, and I couldn't get that man out of my head. Finally I sat up and saw Jake sitting up as well.

"Can't sleep?" he asked.

I shook my head.

"Me neither."

"Why?"

"Nightmares, same as you."

"What do you dream about?"

"Well, mostly the war."

"World War II?" Surprised by his nod, I added, "Pa was in that war."

"Yeah? Which service?"

"Marines. He was a sergeant, jumped out of planes and did some other stuff." I didn't know much about Pa's service. He never would discuss the war with me, always cut off my questions with a single sentence: "That don't concern you, boy." When he said that, it made me absolutely furious, but there was nothing I could do.

"He must be very brave." Jake interrupted my thoughts. "Jumping out of planes is a dangerous assignment. And when you jump in wartime behind enemy lines, it's pretty close to suicide."

Jake's response made me stop and think. I'd never paid much attention to the danger. I'd thought about the glory, the heroism of it. In fact, I'd thought about joining after high school so I could learn to jump from a plane. But Jake's comments put a different twist on things.

"What did you do in the war?"

"I drove a tank."

"Was it fun?"

Jake snorted, but then he reconsidered. "At times. Tanks are slow. You feel like you're inside a giant tortoise, crawling along, and it's difficult to see. But they do protect you from all but the worst shelling. And they're powerful." He smiled. "When I first learned to drive one, I almost felt like Superman..." His smile disappeared, and he sighed.

"Was it dangerous?"

"Yeah, but more so for the infantry, the guys who ran alongside. They didn't have the same kind of protection, were much more likely to get shot."

His version of the war sounded more and more frightening, less the excitement and glory I'd imagined. "Were you hurt?" It was one of those questions I'd asked Pa but had never gotten a reply. I held my breath.

"Not much. I lost some hearing in my ears, and my head got banged up in one big explosion. But I was lucky—got out with no bad burns."

He answered my question! I was so jazzed, I tried another question. "Did you kill a lot of people?"

Jake stayed quiet for some time before he spoke. "Too many. No more questions for tonight. I need to sleep." He turned his back and soon faked a snore.

I must have slept because I woke up to daylight. Jake was gone, and I snuck outside to pee. He returned in a bit with some eggs. "I'll cook these for you, if you want to stick around."

I'd almost forgot I planned to leave, and I gratefully accepted his offer to cook eggs as an excuse to stay awhile.

"There's a spring pump up near that tree next to the farmhouse." Jake pointed up the hill. "They'll let you get fresh water there and wash your face and hands. If you take this container and fill it up for me, I won't charge you for the eggs." He said this with a smile, so I knew he was teasing. I still grabbed the container before trotting up the hill.

The eggs were delicious, cooked soft and spread on a thick piece of bread. I drank a couple glasses of cold spring water and felt full for the first time in days.

"You want to go with me to the farm?" Jake asked. "That's how I pay for eggs and make enough money to buy my other food. All we do is pitch hay to the cattle and put the old straw and manure in the spreader. It's messy work, but once we're finished we can swim."

"Sure!" I was ready for a project, especially one that kept me near to Jake. And today he seemed willing to let me hang around. So we hiked uphill past the spring pump and the farmhouse to an old weathered barn. I'd seen a hundred like it in the country near my home, but I'd never worked on a farm. Maybe if I had, I would not have been as willing.

Jake handed me a shovel and pointed to where the cows stood in stalls, waiting to be fed. "I'll fork hay into their mangers, and you clean up the stuff that comes out the other end."

Holy shit! That expression took on a whole new meaning before the first hour passed. Who would have thought that cows could make so much! I shoveled and threw it into the big spreader until my arms couldn't lift the shovel one more time.

Jake climbed down from the loft. "Good job," he said. "I'll take it from here."

I rested while he finished all the stalls and even redid the ones I'd cleaned. Then he stacked the tools back in the room where he'd found them.

"Ready for a swim?" He led the way up the hill.

By this time the sun blazed in the sky, and a muggy haze cloaked the valley below. Soon as we reached the pond, I stripped down to my shorts and used the rope swing to jump into the middle. The water was clean and cool, more like a swimming hole than your normal farm pond. Above me, I watched a wild stream flow off the Cumberlands and drop several feet into the basin where we swam. Then it slowed and ran across the open fields until it disappeared beneath the road.

After I was clean enough, I went to wash my clothes, and Jake pointed me to a spot further downstream. I nodded and rinsed my clothes out there. Then with all our clothes drying on the rocks, we both lay out and toasted in the sun.

By noon the heat was sweltering, so we dressed in our damp clothes and walked home. As we drew close, I wrinkled up my nose. The dump always smelled like garbage, but today I could see fumes rising from the piles, and the putrid odor made me queasy. I heard a distant buzz that grew loud as we approached. There had to be a billion flies covering the heaps. Their racket combined with the stench and the heat until I felt close to puking.

Jake seemed immune to the smell, but when I lagged behind, he stopped and turned. "Something wrong?"

"It stinks bad!"

"Yeah, it does that in the summer. But today is Wednesday."

I had no idea what that meant, but when I squinted past the dump, I saw a front- loading tractor. As I watched, it crawled from pile to pile, dumping tons of fresh dirt atop the stinking refuse. It took most of the afternoon, and even though the heat progressed, the stench retreated to a tolerable level. I lay down on the sleeping bag and breathed a little deeper. My nausea receded, and eventually I fell asleep.

A dreadful cry woke me. It startled me so bad I wet my pants.

Jake stood in the doorway. *"No!"* he yelled. *"No! It can't be!"* Then he collapsed on the floor. At first I thought he'd been shot, but no sound came from outside, and when I dared to peek, no one was there.

I crawled next to Jake. He was sobbing and banging his head against the plywood. "No," he whispered, "no, no, no, no." He moaned, curled up, and appeared to fall asleep.

I desperately wanted to ask him what just happened, but I didn't dare to wake him. I stepped around his body and walked up to the spring pump for a drink. By the time I got back, he was sitting in the doorway with his head clasped between his hands.

"You okay?" I asked.

He took a deep breath, exhaled, and repeated that behavior several times before saying, "Yeah, I'm great."

That was a lie, and up until now Jake hadn't lied, but then he wasn't acting much like his normal self. I hoped he'd have some explanation. "What happened?"

"Just a dream."

"But your eyes were wide open, and you were standin' up."

"I was?" He wrinkled his brow. "I was up?"

When I told him what he'd done, it upset him so bad, I feared he was going to cry again. I turned away and watched the sun as it traced its path toward the horizon. The sky was too clear to make much of a sunset, and as the fiery disc sank behind the mountains, a cooler breeze blew across my face.

By the time I looked back, Jake had pulled himself together and started wiping dishes off with a dirty towel. His expression turned serious when he saw me.

"We need to talk."

I sat down.

"If I have a nightmare, you can't touch me, okay?"

"Okay." I shrugged.

"Listen, Pete! This is important. Do you promise?"

I didn't understand what was so darn important, but the promise didn't sound that hard to keep. "Okay, I promise."

"On your *life?*"

His tone of voice scared me, capturing my attention. "You're gonna kill me if I touch you?"

"Only in a nightmare—the kind where I'm up walking."

"Like earlier?"

"Yeah, like today."

I recalled how he'd screamed and hit his head. "You're crazy then?"

His jaw muscles clenched, but he sighed. "Probably so. That's why you mustn't touch me."

There was so much pain and sadness in his eyes, I nodded my head and said, "I promise on my life." After that, he let me be.

Jake said nothing more about his nightmare. We ate more beans for supper, this time with ketchup on them, and he let me investigate the contents of the shed. I found a box of tools, a few pieces of clothing, books on carpentry and fishing, a fishing pole, a rifle with no ammo, and some boots. While I satisfied my curiosity, he kept cleaning.

"We need to wash the towels and the blankets," he said, "and judging from the sunset, tomorrow should be perfect weather for it, hot and sunny."

Then it struck me. He expected me to spend another night, and a wave of relief washed over me as I curled up on the floor.

Chapter 3

That night we both slept without any further nightmares. At dawn, we hurried through our chores. Then we returned to the shed, gathered up the towels and bedding, and lugged the laundry to the pond. I asked Jake for soap, but he said it wasn't needed. So we soaked everything, wrung it out, and repeated the soaking and wringing for good measure. After that, we spread all our blankets on the rocks and washed ourselves.

We didn't reach the shed until mid-afternoon. Starved, I spread more beans on bread to make us sandwiches while Jake shared a bag of slightly stale potato chips. After eating, we sprawled out on our beds, and since neither of us felt the least bit sleepy, Jake asked questions.

"When did your ma leave?"

"Two months ago, in June." I paused, unsure how to tell him about Ma. Her life seemed pretty easy, especially since Mamaw did all the cooking and the housework. I couldn't figure out why she felt sad.

Jake looked at me as if he expected a long story. I hadn't meant to tell him about Ma, but as we rested, my mind wandered back.

"It happened on my birthday, the last day of school. When I got off the bus, I felt like nothin' could go wrong."

He smiled.

"But when I got home, there was this big white van parked in our driveway. I ran through the door and collided with two men."

"Who were they?"

"Medics, I guess. They were carryin' my ma out on a stretcher."

Jake frowned. "Did you know she was sick?"

"No." Maybe I should have known; she stayed in bed a lot. But she never looked like she was dying, not until I saw her on the stretcher with eyes closed and face white as ice.

"Was anybody else there?"

"Mamaw. She grabbed me hard—pulled me out of their way."

"And then?"

"They put Ma in the van." I felt strange, as though it was happening right now. I glanced at Jake and caught him watching me intently.

"Did your mamaw tell you what was wrong?"

"No." I shook my head once, trying to escape the eerie sense of being there. "But when she called Pa, I listened in." I hesitated, not certain I should tell him everything, or even if I could. I felt woozy.

Jake studied my face with gentle eyes, as if he knew exactly how I felt. He spoke softly. "It's okay, Pete." It's always okay to tell the truth." His support helped me say the words.

"She sliced her wrists."

As soon as I said it, I felt the shock again. Even having seen her, I'd not realized what she'd done. I remembered clearly what Pa said, his voice high and brittle, like a string stretched to breaking. "She tried to kill herself? Why? Why would she do that? She knows I love her. And the kids. What would make her want to leave her kids?" Even Mamaw couldn't answer that.

Jake was quiet as I stared through the doorway into the late afternoon sun. At any other time, I would have found it soothing. But my chest felt so tight, I fought to breathe. I lay still, listening to the sound of Jake's breathing, and began to match his steady rhythm with my own. Somehow that helped.

Jake waited until I was calm before he spoke. "Has she been there all this time?"

"Yeah."

"Have you seen her?"

"No. Kids can't visit the asylum." That rule pissed me off. Pa went every Saturday, and sometimes Mamaw too, but I hadn't seen my ma in months.

Jake got up and poured himself some water. Then he poured another glass and handed it to me. "Is that why you ran away?"

"Partly." That was as close to the truth as I could get. Of course, if I was home that wouldn't stop me. I'd make up a story just to get them off my back. But I couldn't bring myself to lie to Jake. When he looked inside me with his curious blue eyes, I felt absolutely certain he knew truth from fiction. With him, I didn't even try.

"Why then?"

I shook my head. That truth was so far beyond my understanding I couldn't even fit it in my brain.

To my intense relief, he changed the topic. "It's time for supper. You want beans again, or would you rather go out and eat fried fish?"

I jumped at the chance to go someplace new, so we took off. We didn't have to walk far. Right by the river, we found a roadside diner and stopped there. Jake must have bought our chicken there the first night, because the coleslaw tasted just as good, and I savored every bite of deep-fried trout. We were still lounging at their counter when the setting sun lit the sky with an explosion of red and purple flames.

"Best show on earth," Jake sighed with satisfaction. Then he grinned.

On the walk back, we were quiet for a ways. Jake wrinkled up his brow like he was thinking. We were halfway back before he asked, "So your family has a place in Walnut Springs?"

I nodded.

"And nobody's there?"

"Best I know."

"So where's Mamaw and your sister?"

"At Aunt Kate's."

"And why aren't you with them?" He raised an eyebrow like a furry question mark.

I stared past him, down the road. "I tricked 'em into leavin' home without me."

"What'd you do?"

"I said I was sleepy and lay down in the car. But as soon as they both went in the house, I piled lots of stuff 'neath my blankets and took off."

Jake frowned and studied my face closely. "How far you think they got before they missed you?"

"Probably closer to Nashville than to home." Since Sarah and Mamaw weren't speaking to me then, they wouldn't try to wake me until they stopped for gas. They probably didn't stop 'til well past Cookeville.

"When they found you missing, what do you think they did?" Jake stopped walking, his blue eyes piercing mine.

I turned away. "They went back and looked for me, I reckon."

Jake nodded. "Yeah, that's what I figured. And I bet they're still searching high and low. The least you could do is give your aunt a call."

"I don't know her number." Even as I spoke, it sounded like a pitiful excuse.

By the time we reached the hill, the sunset clouds had merged overhead, blotting out the moon and stars. We finished our walk in total darkness. Jake went inside to light the lantern, and I moseyed near the dump to pee. When I came inside, Jake was resting on his bed.

"Tomorrow after work, we'll walk to town and *find* her number. Which means we'll get up really early. Get some sleep."

His calm, deep voice left no room for argument, but his ultimatum made it difficult to sleep. Luckily the fried fish and coleslaw seemed to help. I didn't even dream—that I remember.

Dawn rose hot and humid, and we hurried through our chores so we could swim. Afterward Jake rushed me to the shed. He made me comb my hair, though his was matted beyond combing, and we retraced our steps past the fish place into town.

Harriman resembled Walnut Springs in many ways. Both main streets stretched less than a mile down the highway. But Harriman had a hospital, and close by the river I saw two industrial-type buildings. In the main part of town, we found a local diner and stopped in there to get a drink. The ladies behind the counter let us choose a table and brought us each a Coca-Cola and a straw. They didn't seem upset with our appearance, so I guessed they either knew Jake or they simply weren't as fussy as my ma.

"You got a Nashville phone book?" Jake asked once he'd paid.

"Naw, not here. But the City Library next to the City Building does."

We found the City Library right across the street. When we walked in, Jake received some worried stares. He didn't seem to notice and asked for the phone book at the reference department. The lady there smiled and handed it to him.

"Do you know her last name?" he asked me.

"I think it's the same as Ma's maiden name, Hansen."

Jake thumbed quickly through the pages to Hansen. He found a K. Hansen in downtown Nashville and another listed in Mount Juliet. "That sounds right," I said. He copied down the number and address and then asked where we could use a phone.

Next thing I knew, he handed me the phone, and I was talking to a very emotional Aunt Kate.

"My God, Pete, where are you? Everyone's been frantic! Your pa called the police, and your mamaw and I have lived by the telephone for days. Are you all right?"

"I'm fine," I said, unimpressed by her dramatics. No one seemed to give a darn *before* I ran away. "I'm stayin' with a friend."

"We called Lee's parents, and they hadn't seen you! Where are you?"

"With a new friend named Jake. He lives outside of Harriman."

"Do his parents know you're there?"

"Yeah." That was my first outright lie, but it wouldn't do to tell her the whole truth.

"Are they treating you right? Do you have enough to eat?"

"Oh, yeah." That part was the truth.

"So do you plan to stay there?"

Her hopeful tone of voice made me so furious I said, "Sure."

"Can I speak with his parents?"

"No, they don't have a phone. I walked into town just to call you."

"Oh. Well. Tell them to call *me*." Her voice turned cold and snooty, a reminder of why I hated her.

"Okay," I said, and I hung up.

Jake raised an eyebrow at the brief conversation. "Well?"

"She's not in any rush to see me."

"They know where you are?"

"More or less, and that's as much as Aunt Kate wants to know."

He frowned. I knew right then he wanted me to leave, but I didn't relish staying with Aunt Kate. I waited with my fingers crossed for Jake to say the words.

"You can't stay here." The tension in his voice squelched my hopes, but I couldn't make myself pick up the phone. Jake sighed, redialed, and gave me the receiver.

This time Mamaw answered. "Hi, Pete. I'm really glad you called us back."

"They want me to go home."

Mamaw sighed. "We don't have a car—your pa has it. Is there a bus or a train from there to Nashville?"

I turned to Jake. "Mamaw wants to know if there's a bus or a train."

"Yeah. There's a train yard about a mile down the highway. It costs five dollars for a ride to Nashville."

"Train," I said to Mamaw. "But it costs five bucks. I could walk."

"Don't be silly, I'll send the money. Do you have their address?"

I asked Jake, and he pulled out a paper with his post office box number scrawled across the top. I read it aloud over the phone.

"Come home soon," Mamaw said, and she almost sounded like she meant it.

Chapter 4

Jake and I walked another mile down the highway just so I could see the railroad yard, a huge field covered with crisscrossed tracks and lights.

The hint of a smile lit Jake's face. "They don't have passenger trains here."

I stared at him, mouth open. "Then how will I get there?"

"You'll ride a freight. I traveled all over North America on freights. And here in the countryside, they'll let about anyone ride for a small fee. Of course it's not strictly legal, so don't go bragging to your friends."

I knew that was meant to cheer me up, but it wasn't that easy for me to change my mood, so I stayed silent. We hiked to the post office, where Jake picked up his mail. He sorted through the letters and stuck them in his pocket before he turned to me and said, "It'll be September in a couple more weeks. I bet your sister and pa will come back to Walnut Springs, maybe even your ma. Your whole family could be there before school starts."

I hung on his words, hoping they were true, until he mentioned the word "school." I'd almost forgot that ugly fact.

They failed me in fourth grade, so now I'd be repeating. That thought stole the smile from my face.

Jake turned to me and raised an eyebrow. "School's not *that* bad. Is it?"

"You don't know. Last year I messed up my schoolwork somethin' awful. So this year I have to do it over, like a retard."

"Why'd you fail?"

I shrugged, too depressed to discuss it further. My feet were dragging when we reached the grocery store.

While Jake bought groceries, I rummaged through a stack of comic books. I had my *Superman* comic in my pocket, but I discovered a *GI Joe* I really wanted. Jake found me sitting on the floor, reading. "I'll buy that, if you like."

I tossed it in his cart and followed him to the checkout.

"I bought us some real food," he said. I saw fresh green beans, potatoes, and apples. He'd not bought any meat, but I was too miserable to question his food choices. I could already hear my old friends at school cracking retard jokes behind my back. And I couldn't make new friends. The kids in my class would be too small!

Jake didn't comment on my problems with school as he turned off the highway and stepped inside a wooden shack with a crawdad and worm hand drawn on its sign. I half smiled and glanced up at his face. He chose a white cardboard box and tossed a dime onto the counter.

"We're goin' fishin'?" I asked, scared he'd say no, tell me I was too young, or some other dumb excuse.

He just nodded and smiled down at me. "You like to fish?"

"Yeah!" My mind jumped to fishing with my pa. Behind our house, you could hike right through the woods to a deep creek filled with overgrown catfish. Pa taught me how to set up my line, cast it in a good spot, and sit real still. It was hard waiting for a fish, but I knew to act quick once it bit because unless you set the hook with a good firm tug, that fish was gone.

We walked back to the shed, and Jake set the groceries on the table. Then he went to the back corner and pulled out a long pole, extra fishing line, and hooks. He set those by the door and wandered down into the dump. I watched, puzzled, as he searched the newest piles and pulled a bamboo pole from a rusty garbage can. He brought it back.

"I saw this the other day and thought it might prove useful." He nailed some arched staples to its length and slid the line underneath so you could pull it easy. Then he finished the other end with another length of line and a hook. When he handed me the fishing pole, I grinned.

"Come on." Jake picked up his stuff. "Let's catch some fish."

We hiked up the hill to the swimming pond and rock-climbed above the little falls. There the creek ran faster, rushing between boulders. We climbed farther up the mountain until Jake said, at last, "This is a good place for trout." He pulled a mayfly from the little cardboard box and carefully tied it to the hook. Then he cast into the deepest part and flicked the line across the surface of the water. His lure moved like a real fly, zigzagging toward a rocky overhang. With a twist of his wrist, he darted his fly under the rock, out again, and then back under.

A trout struck, and Jake hooked him good. Then the real fight began. Without a fancy spinner on his rod, Jake faced a challenge. Pa would have let his line out, but Jake had to run along the creek to keep his catch. The fish dove, jumped, and then dove again. The line grew taut, and the rod bent from the strain. Jake was struggling up some rocks when he slipped; his line went slack.

"Damn!" Jake shut his mouth tight and climbed down to where I stood. We hiked back to where we started, and he tied on another line, hook, and fly. "You want to try?"

"I never learned to fish that way."

He shrugged and managed a wry smile. "Maybe your approach will work better."

I picked a place upstream, dug a worm for my hook, and cast my line near a likely spot. The current picked it up and moved it downstream pretty fast, so I walked down and found the box of bait. "Can I use one of these?"

Jake nodded and showed me how to tie it to the hook. I thanked him and climbed back to my spot. I tried to mimic his moves, but all I really did was catch my hook on some driftwood. I rescued my bait and tried again. With practice, I began to learn, though my lure didn't move as smooth and natural as his. At least I kept it moving on the surface of the water for a short time. Worn out, I laid my fishing pole across a rock and stretched.

Bam! A fish bit. I ran to set the hook. "Got one!" I yelled as the fish began to fight. It wasn't very big, but that turned out to be a plus since it didn't fight all that long. I soon brought it in where I could grab it. Triumphant, I carried it downstream to the stringer.

Jake was nowhere to be seen. I peered up and down the creek but couldn't spot him. I waited, fished a little more, caught another trout, and then lay back on a rock. The sun neared the mountaintop and it would soon be dark, but I was happy. Evening was a good time to fish, and I guessed Jake was luring trout downstream. I waited and waited. The whippoorwills began to call, and later still a barred owl hooted far off in the woods.

I was half-asleep when Jake returned. He didn't have his fishing pole, much less any fish, and he swayed a little as he walked.

"Where you been?" I asked.

"Catch anything?" His voice grated, low and gruff. I pulled out the stringer with my two small trout and a wave of relief crossed his face. "Good for you. Let's take them home and clean them."

Jake was acting strange, so I didn't question him a second time. We hiked down the mountain, past the pond and barn and farmhouse, and stopped at the spring pump where he cleaned both my fish. It was really late when we got back to the shed, but Jake lit the lantern and sent me to find wood. When I returned, he'd chopped up the potatoes and green beans and put them in a pot. I got the fire going, and he set the pot to boiling on a grill over the flames. Once it bubbled and steamed, he laid the trout across the grill.

I watched his face in the flickering firelight. At first he looked totally pissed off, and that scared me. Then he changed to that far away stare I'd seen before. But when the trout was almost ready, I saw him flash a smile, and then I let myself relax.

Once the cooking was done, I brought out plates and forks, and we sat by the fire to enjoy our feast. The fish could have been a little bigger, and the green beans were too crunchy, but all in all, it tasted good.

Jake didn't talk much while we ate, and I wondered if this would be his mood until I left. But after we wiped the dishes clean and stacked them, he became his curious self again. He placed the lantern on the tabletop and picked up the comic book he'd bought. "Can you read this?"

"Sure."

"Read it aloud." He slapped the bed next to him, and I moved to where we both could see the pictures.

As I read, I gave each character a slightly different voice, like Ma used to do in some hazy memory. That made him smile. But when the action scenes grew bloody, he turned away with a frown.

"You read well," he said once I was done. "Why didn't you pass your grade?"

I shrugged, but Jake raised an eyebrow. I knew what that meant and explained. "There's so much stupid work you gotta do, just so, and I never could seem to get it right."

Jake gave me a puzzled look, kind of like my pa did when he asked the same question.

"Have you always had a problem?"

"No, just last year."

"Bad teacher?"

"Maybe." I tried to think about Miss Clausen and instantly felt uncomfortable and dumb. "I couldn't understand her, couldn't please her, and everything I tried to do seemed to make her angry. But all the other kids did okay."

Jake frowned as he listened. "Were things rough at home?"

I shrugged again, and Jake shot me an exasperated frown. Reluctantly, I struggled to explain. "Ma was worse, but then she was pregnant, and Pa was gone most of the time. And when he *was* home, he kept gripin' about money, her doctor bills, and all that kinda stuff."

Jake nodded, although he crinkled his eyebrows as if puzzled. But unlike my family, he didn't seem to blame me for my failure. Instead he approached it like an unsolved mystery, investigating clues to find the cause.

Late that night I relaxed atop my blankets, puzzling on a different mystery. Where did Jake go while we were fishing? Why wouldn't he tell me? What made him so mad? I might have figured he was drunk, but there were no bottles in his shed. He acted much the same with that scary waking dream, right before he warned me not to touch him. Could he dream while he was fishing?

Chapter 5

The next couple days I followed Jake's routine. We awoke early, worked hard at the farm, went swimming, and napped in the middle afternoon. After that we talked, cooked, and read some every night. But we never fished again, and I never got the courage to ask Jake what happened.

The dreaded day finally arrived. We did our chores early, and Jake told me to wash extra well in the pond. After that we walked into town. Mamaw had done just as she promised, and the money was waiting in Jake's post office box, so he and I hiked the mile to the train yard.

We had less than an hour to say goodbye. Jake was very quiet, and by now I suspected he'd miss me. But I doubted he'd miss me half as much as I'd miss him. I'd told at least one truth on the phone. Jake was my friend.

Too soon the freight train rumbled through the yard and hissed loudly to a stop. Jake led me past the coal cars and boxcars to the very end. "Hey, Harper," he yelled to a large, gray-haired man dressed in a railroad uniform.

"Hey, Jake!" The man jumped to the ground and grabbed Jake in a bear hug. "You going traveling?"

"No, just my friend. Pete, this is Harper. He'll get you to Mount Juliet in one piece and probably fill your ears with tall tales on the way."

Harper reached out and shook my hand. "Jump up on the rear platform; I'll be there in a jiff."

"Do exactly what he says," Jake added with his blue-eyed stare.

I climbed up onto the platform and sat quietly while he spoke with his friend. Then Jake walked back to me. From where I sat, I could look straight into his eyes, and the corners drooped like a hound dog's.

"I enjoyed your visit, more than you know. You're a good kid, and you're plenty smart enough, in spite of school. I hope your pa and ma get their lives straightened out so you can have a family. If that fails, you know where to find me." Then much to my surprise, he reached over, hugged me, and walked off without a single backward glance.

As I watched Jake leave, my stomach felt real empty. I almost climbed down and followed him, but before I could move, Harper joined me. "We'll pull out any time now, just sit tight." Then he jumped off the other side and disappeared again. My stomach lurched when the train began to move, but just as we were leaving, Harper jumped aboard. "You're goin' to Mount Juliet?"

"Yes, sir."

"Ever been there before?"

"I've been to Aunt Kate's, outside of town."

"Not much of a town, if you ask me. Nashville's some better. But if you want a city, you gotta see Chicago. That's a real city—big, busy, and brimming with opportunity. What d'you wanna be?"

I shrugged. "What made you wanna work on trains?"

He scratched his head. "I guess where I lived. Out on the plains there's nothing except space, lots of open prairie. The train tracks stretch all day to the horizon. When I was your age, I thought for certain I'd find treasures at the end—had to go." He smiled.

I smiled back. "I'd like to see flat land. I've always lived in a valley where the mountains pen you in."

Harper nodded as he studied me. "You might be a traveler, like Jake. He could make good money if he ever settled down, but he won't."

"Why not?"

Harper shrugged. "Because he's Jake."

We picked up speed as we headed for the mountain. The tracks paralleled the highway for a bit and then took a turn. There weren't many houses up this way, mostly trees with the occasional shack or tiny farm. We stopped very briefly at Crab Orchard, and past there the train slowed for a steady uphill climb. In less than an hour, we pulled into Crossville.

"I gotta work—be right back." Harper hopped off.

When he returned, I asked, "What do you do?"

"I'm a brakeman. I check and set the brakes and couplings on the cars, and I throw switches on the tracks. The switches control which track the trains use. At each stop, some cars are backed onto sidetracks and uncoupled from the front part of the train. They may hook up with other trains or stay there to be unloaded. Feel that bump? That's the front end hitching up with us again. Now we can leave."

I must have dozed with the clatter of the wheels and the rumble of the engine lulling me to sleep. When Harper woke me and told me Mount Juliet was next, I sat up and ran my fingers through my hair, tucked my shirt into my jeans, and tied my shoes. By the time we slowed for the station, I was ready.

"You're lucky, they're gonna stop today," Harper said. "But not for long. Jump off when I do and run straight across the yard toward the road. No other trains should be coming. Understand?"

I nodded, and as soon as he landed, I jumped down and ran across a bunch of railroad tracks. Once I reached the road, I turned around and looked. Harper was watching, and he waved.

I felt pretty good. I'd gotten to Mount Juliet with just a little help, and it couldn't be that far to Aunt Kate's. I saw a filling station near the tracks and walked inside. The lady at the counter asked, "What you need?"

"I need to get here," I pulled out Jake's paper with Aunt Kate's address and phone number and discovered a one-dollar bill wrapped in its folds. A gift from Jake! I wanted to grin and cry at the same time.

"You want me to call them—have them come pick you up?" the lady asked.

"They don't have a car. But I can walk."

She ruffled through some papers until she found a map. Then she laid it on the counter and searched to find the house. "Got it," she said, marking the spot with an X. "Can you read a map?"

"Kinda."

She placed the map upside down on the counter. "You go out the front door and turn right." She pointed left. "Go to the light and turn left." She pointed right. "That's a big street with lots of shops. You're gonna follow it a long ways, several miles. But here you turn right on Linden Way, and her house is on a private road, almost a mile on the left."

I reached for the map, but she shook her head. "It's not mine to give away. Just remember what I told you. It ain't hard."

Suddenly I was back in school with Miss Clausen who spouted out orders I couldn't understand. I panicked, grabbed the map, and ran. Still running when I hit the main street, I crossed it and turned opposite the tracks.

After a few more blocks I slowed, and no one noticed. The sun was setting, and all the people on the streets were headed home for supper. I was hungry too and realized that I wouldn't reach Aunt Kate's house until late. I walked faster.

It took several hours just to reach Linden Way, a quiet road that wandered through the country. I had less than a mile left to go, but I'd started my day shoveling cow shit at dawn, and now my feet were hurting, my stomach was growling, and I couldn't force my legs to take one more step. I should have eaten earlier, before the stores all closed.

I curled up near the road and must have nodded off. A bright light startled me awake. When I opened my eyes and couldn't see, I tried to run. A man grabbed my shoulder and threw me face down on the ground. It wasn't until he started reading me my rights that I figured out he was a cop. I hated cops! I hated all men carrying guns. But I knew better than to argue.

He cuffed me and pulled me to my feet. "What's your name, boy?"

"Pete Martin."

"What ya doin' here?"

"I'm walkin' to Kate Hansen's house. It's just a little further up the road."

"You know the address?"

"It's in my pocket." I nodded to my right pocket, which held Jake's note, and prayed he didn't find the stolen map in the left.

The cop pulled out the note and read it. He continued to eye me with suspicion. "I know the lady there, and she don't have no kids."

I put on my most innocent expression. "I'm her nephew, and I just arrived."

He looked me up and down, having every reason to question what I said. I looked more like a hobo than nephew to a well-bred, Christian lady.

"Well, Pete, it's a long shot, but for now you can ride shotgun in the squad car. Then we'll see what Miss Hansen has to say."

I didn't much like it, but what else could I do? I climbed into the front seat and forced a smile. The car quickly covered the next dozen blocks and pulled into a driveway. I'd not visited Aunt Kate in several years, but the two-story farmhouse with its wide front porch brought a pleasant memory to mind. Two years back, I sat on the porch swing with both Ma and Pa, searching the sky for shooting stars. At least I'd come to the right place.

The cop got out, opened my door, and escorted me up the steps. He didn't remove the cuffs until he knocked.

After several minutes, Aunt Kate cracked the door. She was a shorter, stiffer version of my ma, with her blond hair pulled back and pale, watery blue eyes. Those eyes stared at me through bifocal lenses as if she didn't know who I might be. I could sense the cop readying himself to take me in, but then Aunt Kate connected all the dots.

"Pete, is that you?"

I nodded.

"Lord, help me! You've changed so in the last two years, I wouldn't have known you at all."

She waved and smiled at the cop, who waved back and climbed into his car. By this time, Mamaw and Sarah blocked the doorway. I thought they'd never let me in. Finally Aunt Kate got the chain off the door and opened it barely enough for me to enter. I collapsed on the couch, took off my shoes, and started rubbing on my feet.

Aunt Kate and Mamaw exchanged a worried glance. I trusted Mamaw's judgment a lot more than Aunt Kate's, but this was Aunt Kate's house, and she got first say. As usual, she assumed the worst.

"What are you doing here at this time of night? And why were you riding with that cop? Are you in trouble?"

"Naw." I kept my expression calm. "It was a long walk from the train, and I got tired. He saw me sittin' and offered me a lift."

Mamaw nodded and slowly climbed the stairs. She wore her nightie, and her gray hair hung loose down her back. I guessed she was asleep when I arrived.

I turned to Aunt Kate. "Can I have supper? I'm starved."

Aunt Kate stared at me as if she'd just bitten into something bitter. Reluctantly she made her way into the kitchen and produced a sandwich with one thin slice of ham. I gulped it down.

"It's midnight," she said.

"Yeah, thanks."

"We weren't expecting you," she continued. "I don't have a place for you to sleep."

"That's okay. I can sleep here on the sofa."

"Goodness no, that would never do. Wait here while I make up a bed."

I wanted to tell her that up until tonight, I'd slept on the floor of a stinky, one- room shack, but I knew that wouldn't change her mind. So I smiled politely and helped myself to milk and cookies.

Sarah joined me in the kitchen. She looked like a smaller, teenage version of Ma, except with blue-green eyes and dark blond hair. She wore PJs. First she glanced at the parlor to make sure Aunt Kate and Mamaw were upstairs, and then she began talking in a whisper. "You have no idea what you've gotten yourself into. Our whole family's in a mess. Ma's medical bills have ate up all our funds. Pa is workin' overtime on nights. He sold his car—that's why he's driving ours—and he might even have to sell our house."

Her last statement caught my whole attention. "Sell our house? You're kiddin'."

"No, I'm not. That's what he told Mamaw when he called."

She didn't admit to listening on the phone, but I'd learned that trick from her, so I believed her. Lose our house? That would be a blow from which we'd never recover. My parents loved that house. In fact the house was the only thing they both worked hard to keep. And with it gone…? I couldn't imagine us living in a shed.

"How's Ma?" I asked.

"Pretty much the same. They talk about lettin' her come home. But only if Pa's there, and that assumes we have a home." Sarah pouted her lips and hung her head.

I suddenly realized my teenage sister felt as abandoned as I did. That surprised me. Sarah always acted self-sufficient and was such a know-it-all that I looked up to her as an adult. Maybe she wasn't as superior as she acted, and with that understanding, I liked her a lot more.

"Thanks for fillin' me in. Is that everythin' I need to know?"

"Everythin' but Lee. He called to find you, and we ended up talkin'—mostly about your disappearance."

"What'd he say?"

"He was worried—thought you might be in trouble. He's really a smart kid, you know…" She stopped right in the middle of her thought, and I could guess what she didn't want to say. If Lee was so smart, why'd he hang out with me, the flunked-out-of- fourth-grade retard? I was just grateful she'd not said it.

"Yeah, I know. And yes, we are good friends in spite of that."

Sarah ignored my pointed comment and sniffed at the milk carton I'd left out on the shelf. She wrinkled up her nose in disgust. "This milk is spoiled. How can you stand to drink it?"

I had to smile. She was her mother's daughter after all. But her attitude silenced me about my stay with Jake. Sarah would never understand.

Chapter 6

I ended up sleeping on a cot in the attic, which was sort of like a closet way up on the third floor. In reality, it was almost the same size as the shed, but I felt cramped, probably 'cause I had to rethink everything I said and did. Spitting in Aunt Kate's house was a crime equivalent to murder.

Aunt Kate presided at the breakfast table, and she eyed me nose to toes when I walked in. "When is the last time you took a bath, child? And those clothes, did you sleep in them last night?"

"That's all I got with me." I grabbed some ketchup and stirred it with my scrambled eggs before I sat down to eat.

"Mom." She turned to Mamaw. "Did you bring clothes for Pete?"

"I let him pack his own stuff."

Aunt Kate rolled her eyes and glared at her mother. Then she went back to criticizing me. "You grew too fast. How could anyone expect to keep you in nice clothes? I suppose this means we'll have to buy you new ones."

Mamaw pursed her lips, but I didn't know if she was angry with Aunt Kate or with me for not packing and growing out of things. Finally Mamaw nodded. "They both need new school clothes, anyway."

After breakfast, I escaped to the front porch and curled up in the porch swing. For a short time I let myself relax. I was thinking about Lee when Sarah came outside and plopped her bottom down right beside me.

"We need a plan," she said.

"For what?"

"For keepin' the house, stupid."

It was my turn to roll eyes. "What d'you plan to do, rob a bank?"

"Use your brain, if you have one. What is it we really need to do?"

I was clueless, but when Sarah went off on her "superior to thou" kick, she didn't want me to answer anyway. I shrugged.

"Get Ma home, silly. That's where all the money's goin'. If she's home, Pa won't have to work both day and night, and he'll still make enough to keep the house."

Okay, she was older, and smarter, and her ideas weren't half-bad.

"But how? We don't even get to see her."

"I'm goin'." Sarah said this with a simper. "Pa said that once I turned fourteen I could go, and Saturday's my birthday."

I did the math. Sarah's birthday was August 25, 1942. That would indeed make her fourteen on the weekend. It also hit me with the force of a bullet that if Ma stayed forever in the mental asylum, I wouldn't get to see her for close to four more years.

"What's your plan?"

"I'll have to see. If Ma's afraid to leave, I'll just encourage her. But if the doctors want our money, then I'll have to convince them we don't have any left."

"Wouldn't Pa have told them that already?"

Sarah sneered. "Really, Pete. Think! Pa works in mines where no one else will go. Then he buys Ma all those expensive clothes? He's so proud and stubborn; you know he'd rather *die* than tell those fancy doctors that he's broke."

Her comment coincided with something Jake had said—Pa was very brave. Could he be both brave and stupid? That rang a bell. "Okay, you're right. But what about Mamaw? Wouldn't she have told them?"

"I doubt it. She don't do nothin' without first askin' Pa."

That was true—I'd seen it many times. My respect for Sarah surged to a new high.

"It might work," I said, feeling a little hopeful. But a voice inside my head disagreed, *No! Don't bring her home. She hates us!* I recognized all my guilt and anger about Ma and told that stupid voice to shut up. It obeyed, but with a twist to my gut and the distinct feeling that I'd be real sorry later.

"Don't tell them," Sarah added, nodding toward the door as Aunt Kate and Mamaw came outside.

Aunt Kate eyed me with disgust. "Pete, go inside and wash your hands and face, comb your hair, brush your teeth, and tuck in your shirt." She averted her eyes and turned to Mamaw. "He *really* needs a haircut." She rolled her eyes and shook her head. Then she smiled at Sarah. "You look lovely dear. Go get your purse."

Gritting my teeth, I took my own sweet time following every one of her instructions. When I finally descended from the upstairs bath, all three ladies were frowning up at me.

"What took you so long?" Sarah hissed in my ear. Then she smiled sweetly as Aunt Kate led us to the bus stop.

Sarah, Mamaw, and Aunt Kate chatted nonstop all the way. When we reached downtown Nashville, Harvey's was the biggest store we saw, and Aunt Kate directed us to the boys' department. Then she sent me into the dressing room while she picked the clothes—stiff blue jeans and even stiffer button-up, starched shirts. I tried them on, all the while wanting my old soft duds. Mamaw paid the bill, and Aunt Kate beamed as she led me through the store.

"Clothes make the man," she said proudly as she straightened my starched collar. It took all my self-control to smile and say, "Thanks."

Our next stop was the ladies' department. I curled up in a chair and tried hard not to wiggle as each of them grabbed an armful of clothes and disappeared into the dressing room. They oohed and aahed and laughed behind closed doors 'til I was about ready to walk off.

Then Sarah paraded out in a new dress. I stared. It would be a traffic stopper if Pa let her wear it. The blue-green color matched her eyes, and the way it fit made her look— different.

"Like it?" she asked.

"It makes you look more grown up."

That comment seemed to please her, and she flounced back inside.

Soon all three of them emerged with piles of clothes over their arms. This time Aunt Kate paid, and we headed for the street.

Two blocks down the street, we found a barbershop. The ladies left me there while they browsed the other stores. As I held still for the barber, I could see all three of them disappear indoors and reappear again, laughing and talking all the time. The barber made short, and I mean short, work of my hair. I ran my fingers through the prickle and gazed at my image in the mirror. I liked it. It was a genuine military haircut, and it made *me* look more grown up.

When the ladies returned, they stared at my buzzed head. "Well, doesn't he look just like a little soldier," Mamaw said, rubbing on my fuzz.

"It's short," Sarah said, wrinkling up her nose.

Aunt Kate sighed and shook her head. "You better stay away from the prison, boy, or they'll know for sure you're one of theirs." She'd held that opinion of me for some time now, so I paid her no mind.

The last stop was a shoe store. When the salesman measured my big feet, he discovered my old shoes were too small by a whole size. I picked out a pair of black sneakers with white laces. When I walked outside, my feet were smiling.

Our reward for shopping was a trip to the lunch bar down the street. I vaguely remembered the place from years ago, and based on that memory I ordered a root beer float. Mmmmmm, yes! I was in heaven. The ladies, even Sarah, sipped their drinks daintily, but I slurped the last of mine with a loud guzzling noise that caught everyone's attention. Aunt Kate shot me a glare that should've made me duck, but I was too contented.

We rode the bus back, and I returned to the porch swing. I felt good. Sarah was working on a plan to get Ma home, and I looked so different that no one would recognize the filling station map thief. Then the angry voice inside me butted in. *You failed school, stupid. You'll be repeatin' the fourth grade.*

My happy mood dissolved into a puddle of bad feelings. Mamaw had given me some schoolwork to complete. I'd avoided it before I ran, and now it simply was too late. Anyway, I'd *failed*, and that meant I was too stupid to do schoolwork. Maybe I'd grow up both brave and stupid like Pa. I clung to that.

Chapter 7

The week dragged by, and I gave serious thought to running off, this time for good. What kept me from going were my great hopes for the weekend. Pa would be here Friday night. Saturday he'd take Sarah with him to see Ma, and he'd be staying most of Sunday. I was absolutely certain our lives were going to change.

All day Friday I waited on the porch, coming inside only for meals. It was hot, humid, and smelled like rain, but nothing happened until dusk. Then it poured and blew so hard that even underneath the porch roof, I got wet. I started worrying about Pa. Could he drive in this storm? What if the old car died? Would he walk? I almost gave up before I saw the headlights and heard the tires crunch along the gravel. As soon as Pa reached the porch steps, I jumped up.

"Pa!" I hugged him tight, wet clothes and all.

"Hey, Pete, take my coat." He pushed me aside, handed me his coat, and went inside to greet the ladies. I followed, hanging his coat in the closet on the way. By the time I reached the parlor, he was seated on the sofa with Sarah on one side and Mamaw on the other. I pulled up a chair across from them.

He frowned at me. Pa had a way of frowning that made grown men run and hide. He wasn't much more than average tall, with short brown hair and brown eyes, but he could make a bigger man back off in a heartbeat when he frowned.

"I heard you run away, Pete, scairt everyone to death, and didn't even call home for days."

There was nothing I could say. I hung my head.

"That's not okay. You're grounded 'til school starts."

My eyes opened wide. "What?"

"You heard me. Stay in the house or yard. Don't go no further, or I'll have to switch you next."

I couldn't look at him. It hurt too much to see his frown and realize that I'd messed up yet again.

Pa turned to Sarah and complimented her on the new dress. I hated her. She never got caught for listening on the phone, stealing cookies, or trying on Ma's clothes. And if she did, she blamed it all on me. I hated my whole family. Why did I come back?

"Pete?" Mamaw's voice was sharp. "Pay attention. Your pa asked you a question."

I lifted my head.

"Have you caught up on your schoolwork?" he repeated.

I shook my head. "Not really."

"I thought you wanted to get back in the fifth grade?"

I shrugged.

He knitted his brows in a terrifying frown. His voice tightened with anger. "You could try! The rest of us are strugglin' with your ma gone. You could, at the very least, stay out of trouble. I'm workin' day and night just to keep you fed. *Is it so fuckin' hard to do schoolwork?"* I raised my hands to protect my face. Ouch! Too late. My cheek stung and tears sprang to my eyes. He dropped his hand and turned back to the others.

I wanted to leave, but then I'd be a coward. I forced myself to sit there, eyes glued to the floor, until I calmed down enough to listen.

"We'll leave real early in the mornin'. It takes a couple hours to drive down, and then we have to wait for her to come. Sometimes she's ready when I get there, and other times she never shows at all," Pa said. "I just don't want you to take it personal if she's havin' one of those days."

"I understand," Sarah said.

"Be up, dressed, and ready before dawn."

Pa still acted like a sergeant, even though he'd been retired for ten years. He gave the orders and we all obeyed, or if we didn't, he hit us. I mostly got the raw end of his temper, but then I mostly disobeyed.

I glanced at Sarah, and she was all a-shimmer with success. The first part of her plan was playing out as she expected. I almost wished her dead, even though I hoped she would succeed. Maybe, if Ma came home, Pa would treat me better.

No! The angry voice inside my head disagreed. *They hate you. Both of them just hate you. You should leave.* This time I listened and retreated to my bed.

By the time I got up, Pa and Sarah were long gone. At breakfast, Aunt Kate brought me a couple books to read, and I paged through them. The titles were *War and Peace* and *Little*

Women, and they were thick, with small print and no pictures at all. The war book didn't even have much action. I put them both aside and went out in the yard.

If I wanted to run again, I needed to make plans. The first question was, where would I go? I could go to Jake's, but he'd probably send me home. I could jump on a train, head west, and keep on going. Eventually I'd run out of food and money, and no one would pay a kid my age for doing work. Maybe I could change my name and end up in a home for homeless kids. Or get adopted. But I had a bad feeling that wouldn't work out well. I'd probably need to run away again.

I wandered off the property, daring them to stop me, and walked to the bus stop. I had Jake's dollar in my pocket, and I could go anywhere in Nashville for a dime. It wasn't long before a bus pulled in. I climbed aboard, got change, and dropped a dime into the fare box.

I got off downtown, like before, and decided to buy another root beer float. I walked into the food bar, sat down at the counter, and ordered one all by myself. It cost almost a quarter, but it was worth every penny. I caught the next bus back. On a scale of one to ten, that trip scored an eight, almost as good as finding Jake.

By the time I reached the house, Aunt Kate and Mamaw were both cooking. They didn't say anything about my disappearance, even gave me a cookie and some milk. I sat in the kitchen and sniffed sweet aromas 'til I drooled. According to my nose, we were going to eat fried chicken with cornpone, broccoli with cheese, and apple pie for dessert. When I ran away again, I'd sure miss Mamaw's cooking.

Aunt Kate heard the car first. She and Mamaw hurried their food preparations while I ran out to the front porch. Both Sarah and Pa looked wore out, and when I nodded toward the porch swing, Sarah took the hint and stayed. We watched Pa disappear inside.

"What happened? Is she comin' home?" I asked.

Sarah stared at the floor. "I never saw her."

"What? Why not?"

Sarah pouted her lips. "She didn't wanna see me."

I shook my head, though I'd been the butt of Ma's cruelty before. "But why?"

She shrugged. "Pa said maybe she was havin' a bad day and didn't want *me* to see her cryin'."

"What do you think?"

"I think she doesn't want to come back home."

"Did she talk to Pa?"

"No."

I felt bad for my sister. She'd been looking forward to this visit all summer, and Ma just shot her down. Not knowing how to help, I went inside.

All three adults were sitting at the table. I stopped to listen, but they were talking about Ma, and I already knew what happened there. Since I was real hungry, I announced my presence. "Is supper ready yet?"

They all looked up and seemed relieved to see me. "We were just about to put it on the table," Mamaw said. She gave Aunt Kate a stare that put her on her feet and moving fast into the kitchen.

Pa narrowed his eyes. "What d'you do today?"

"Nothin' much."

Pa frowned, but the promise of food distracted him. We all gathered around the table. He said grace, and silence followed as we stuffed food into our mouths. I noticed that Sarah didn't eat, and nobody else had much to say. I thought about asking the adults to make a plan. They must know Ma needed to come home. But something in their silence acted as a warning, and I decided not to chance it.

That night Pa came upstairs to my room. "You disobeyed," he said. "Pull down your pants."

Half asleep, I quietly obeyed. He took off his belt and hit me 'til I yelped.

"Don't push me," he warned, "or you'll get worse."

Once he left, I took extra time with my prayers. I asked Lord Jesus to forgive me for not studying and running off and making Pa so mad. Then I asked him to help Ma come back home. I ended by asking him to be kind to Sarah, 'cause she was just trying to get our family back together. Eventually, I went to sleep.

I dreamed the same nightmare, and when that man put his gun up to my head, I still screamed. That woke me, and Jake wasn't there to talk with, so I got out of bed and walked around. As I was pacing up and down the attic room, I noticed the chimney bricks continued up the wall. I put my ear next to the bricks, and sure enough, I could hear the grownups downstairs. Grabbing a blanket and pillow off the bed, I curled up next to the chimney and listened.

The next day was Sunday. Pa left early, and the four of us walked over to the local church. On the way, I whispered *pssst* at Sarah. She ignored me. Aunt Kate's church was Baptist, while ours was Methodist, but except for the lack of stained glass windows, they looked and sounded pretty much the same. On the walk home, I tried again. But Sarah was still in a funk and kept away.

At dinner, the four of us ate leftovers together. After we ate, I pinched Sarah hard, and then she chased me out onto the porch. Finally!

"I heard somethin' new last night," I said.

Sarah glared at me, still angry from the pinch.

"Mamaw and Pa were talkin' in the parlor."

"How could *you* hear them?" She rolled her eyes in disbelief.

"Through the chimney—it goes up by my room."

Her eyes opened wide, and she sat down on the swing.

"We're goin' home." I grinned.

"Home? To Walnut Springs?" "Yep."

"When?"

"I don't know for sure. But sometime before school starts 'cause that's where we'll be goin' back to school."

Sarah sighed in satisfaction, and I felt a little better. At least my eavesdropping was a useful sin.

"Maybe Ma will come back once we're home," Sarah said.

I knew she was dreaming. And I would've let her dream except that ugly voice inside me said, *You caused this. And nothin' will get better 'til you either run away or die.* I tried hard not to listen, but when something's inside you, how do you ignore it?

56

I yelled at Sarah. "You fool! Ma's *never* comin' home. Get used to it. She hates you and Pa and me most of all. She wants to leave so bad she tried to *die!*"

Sarah burst into tears and ran into the house. Mamaw came outside, hands on her hips. "What is wrong with you, Pete? You think Sarah isn't hurt enough? You think you need to throw it in her face? Go to your room until suppertime—and *think!*"

I obeyed, but I didn't need to think. I knew I was evil, or at least the voice inside of me was headed straight to hell. As I sat on my cot and stared at the brick chimney, for a time I understood how Ma must have felt—sometimes it'd be easier to die.

On Monday, I managed to stay inside the yard. The next day I simply couldn't stand it. I found a bus schedule and checked out all the routes. Unfortunately, there was no bus to Harriman. Instead, I rode downtown and stayed all day, wandering through the streets and browsing through the stores. I even found the Grand Old Opry house where— Mamaw told me—Ma once sang. When I got home, Mamaw said nothing, but this time I knew her silence was a lie. The true reckoning wouldn't come until the weekend, so every day I took a different bus.

Friday came, and we all waited up for Pa, but at eleven p.m. he still wasn't there. Mamaw pursed her lips, and I holed up in my room. I might have run, but I'd used up all my money.

Right around midnight, I thought I heard a car. After a bit, I put my ear to the chimney, and sure enough, I heard Pa talking to Aunt Kate.

"A tree fell on the roof, and it's in bad shape. I gotta replace it before we can move in."

That set my mind to puzzling on a whole new set of worries. Could Pa fix our roof? When would he have the time? Or the money? I asked Lord Jesus for his help. I really begged. In fact it was the mightiest prayer I ever prayed.

Chapter 8

Pa didn't visit me that night. The next morning, he and Mamaw left at dawn for Chattanooga. Since Sarah and I weren't on speaking terms right then, I was left to worry on my own. Pa and Mamaw returned in time for supper, and they happily reported that Ma talked with them all day and even made plans for coming home. Sarah gave me her "right as always" look, but I had doubts. Ma's moods were as changeable as a rollercoaster, and next week she'd sing a different tune.

Pa got our attention at the table and made an announcement that totally surprised me. He'd arranged for two-weeks' vacation from his job so he could fix our roof and move us home. That brought smiles all around. I guess everyone was wondering where he got the money, but only Aunt Kate dared to ask.

"Rob, you told me it takes everything you make to pay the bills. Where did you find money for the roof?"

I'd never seen Pa squirm—until then. He wiggled in his chair, looked down at his food, and his face developed a peculiar rosy color. But he answered her question fair and square. "I took out a loan, a second loan against the house. I figured the house warn't worth much without a roof, and I needed money to buy shingles."

Aunt Kate raised an eyebrow, and I knew what she was thinking. Pa would need more money to pay off both the loans, and he couldn't work longer hours. We were going to lose our house for sure.

Mamaw disagreed. "That house was your inheritance, and you've both worked too hard to fix it up. You have to roof it."

Pa gave Mamaw a nod, although he still looked anxious. When he turned his eyes on me, I held my breath.

"Pete, you're comin' with me to fix the roof."

I was so astonished no words came.

"Now that's settled," he said. "I hope you kids are packed. School starts the first week in September." He turned to Mamaw next. "Are you comin'?"

That question surprised me more than anything I'd heard. Mamaw was family, why wouldn't she come? I glanced over, but she was staring down, her fingers tightly clasped in her lap. I saw her lips move and realized she was praying. Then she looked up, straight at Pa. "Okay, Rob, I'll come with Sarah, but only until Helga gets home and takes over. You know I can't keep doing this forever."

My heart skipped a beat. It never had occurred to me that Mamaw might leave. Even if Ma came home, it wouldn't be the same. Ma hated me. In my mind, I replayed what Mamaw said—she would come with *Sarah*. Next week I'd be all alone with Pa.

After supper, I ran upstairs and gathered up my clothes, old and new, and the few belongings I'd carried with me. I stuck my *Superman* comic deep inside my pocket along with my little flag. Then I leaned against the chimney, waiting for the grown-ups, but instead of listening, I fell fast asleep.

This dream was a doozy. Jake and I were floating down the river in his shed when a storm came up and threatened to drown us. We were rowing hard, but a gigantic waterfall roared up ahead, and no matter what we did, the current won. Our shed disappeared over the edge, and I couldn't find Jake. But somehow I was standing on the riverbank with Pa, and he said, "That's what happens when you don't fix the roof."

I woke up with my neck in a cramp, and it took me several minutes to stretch and rub it out. I couldn't guess the time, but no voices murmured down below. As I lay on my cot, I thought about the dream and wondered about Jake. I wanted to see him, but this week I was stuck with helping Pa.

Before dawn, Pa woke me. "Get up, Pete. I see your stuff's all ready. Get dressed while I throw it in the car."

I jumped up, peed, washed, and dressed in two minutes. Then I ran down both flights of stairs. Mamaw served me hotcakes with warm maple syrup. Yummmy! But I couldn't give them the attention they deserved. Pa was in too much of a hurry.

Mamaw gave me a big hug on the porch, but she pursed her lips tight as we were leaving, and the cramping in my gut told me I was worried too. After all my wandering, Pa would give me trouble. And there would be no chance to run away.

Pa drove the same as he did everything, fast and accurate as a racecar driver. He didn't need me to read the map. He'd memorized the roads and flew through all the lights as if they'd been timed just for him. The sun rose before us as he raced the switchbacks down the mountain and took the local highway through Harriman toward home. I recognized the City Building, library, and diner. Of course, those reminded me of Jake. I couldn't erase that silly dream from my memory, so I said a little prayer to Lord Jesus and asked him to look out for my friend.

The drive from Harriman to Walnut Springs took just over thirty minutes, where it'd taken me a good two days on foot. I craned my neck to peer around the last curve and stared at the roof with our oak tree splayed across it. That tree must have fallen in the very same storm that led me to Jake's shed, which meant the hail and rain had caused more damage.

Our house didn't have a big front porch like Aunt Kate's, but inside it looked pretty much the same. When you walked in the front door, you could see the stairs with the dining room and kitchen over to the right and the parlor and sunroom on the left. At the top of the stairs stood the bathroom with a bedroom at each corner of the house. And up a steeper set of stairs, the smaller attic area doubled as a guest and storage room.

"We're here," Pa said as we drove into the driveway, and those were the first words he'd uttered the whole trip. "I moved all the furniture downstairs, where it's dry. You'll sleep in the dinin' room, and I'm in the parlor."

I opened the front door and stood staring at the mess. I could barely remember how it used to be arranged, but I knew Mamaw always kept it neat. As Pa said, he'd crammed all our beds and dressers in between the sofas, chairs, and eating tables.

I wormed between pieces of misplaced furniture until I found my bed and placed my belongings on it. Pa hadn't come inside, so I went out to find him.

"Help me with the ladder," he yelled as soon as I appeared. He was dragging the longest one we owned from the barn, so I ran and picked up the other end. It was made of wood and weighed a ton, but I lugged my end over to the house. He motioned me away as he rotated the ladder up against the house. "Get some gas and oil for the chainsaw."

I ran back to the barn and brought the cans.

Pa used what he needed and then climbed atop the roof with his saw. He started cutting pieces off the tree. Once he'd sawed off several chunks, he yelled, "I'm gonna throw these down over there. Stay away."

I watched from a distance as he dragged and threw the heavy branches off the roof. When the pile on the ground reached well above my head, he climbed down and cut the limbs into firewood. Then he climbed up and repeated the procedure. It took several hours to remove the whole treetop, and the trunk took several hours more. My job was to stack all the firewood into neat piles by the porch. By the time I'd finished, I wanted to lie down, but Pa was just warming up.

"Get the big tarp and the hammer and some nails—they're on top of my work bench."

I dragged out the tarp. When I came back with the hammer, Pa was drinking from the hose. He offered it to me, and I guzzled down a gallon. The afternoon was warm, and I'd worked up quite a sweat.

"Take a break while I fasten this tarp over the holes." Pa grabbed the tarp, stuck the hammer in his belt, pocketed the nails, and ran back up the ladder.

I leaned against the barn. The sound of his hammer beat a rhythm in my brain, and I started to feel sleepy. The next thing I knew, Pa was shaking me again. "No time to sleep. We need shingles."

I climbed into the car, and he drove to the Co-op. But even on the drive, he didn't rest. "If each side of that roof measures thirty feet by twenty feet, and one square of shingles will cover one hundred square feet, how many squares do we need?"

I stared blankly, and he frowned. "Okay, let's break it down." He drew a rectangle shape in the air. "Suppose this is one side of the roof. The distance from the top to the bottom is twenty feet, and the distance from one end to the other is thirty feet. If you multiply those numbers, you'll have the number of square feet on that side of the roof."

The light came on in my brain. I did the math. "Six hundred."

"But there's two sides to the roof."

"Twelve hundred."

He nodded. "Okay, now shingles are sold in squares, and each square covers one hundred square feet. So how many squares do we need?"

That was easy. "Twelve."

"Exactly right, except we'll need some extra for the ridge and the edges." He turned and glared at me. "Why can't you do that well at school?"

I shrugged.

Chapter 8

At the Co-op, I stayed inside the car while Pa checked out the shingles. He paid and arranged for their delivery the next day and returned carrying tarpaper and nails. Our next stop was the grocery where he bought us stuff for supper. At home, Pa baked potatoes and warmed peas. Then he fried some hamburger, mixed it up with ketchup, and spooned that over bread. My stomach had been growling for an hour, so I thanked him.

"You get to do the dishes," he said.

I took a dishcloth and wiped the dishes clean.

"Damn it, Pete, you got a lazy streak a mile wide. You have to wash 'em first." He filled up one side of the sink with hot water, squirted in some soap, and put the dishes in the suds. "Wash 'em on this side, rinse the soap off on the other, and stack 'em in the rack so they can dry."

I thought Jake's approach was much simpler, but Mamaw always did them like Pa said. I carefully washed, rinsed, and stacked all the dishes, and by the time I finished, Pa was sleeping.

Pa shook me awake before the sun rose. "Get dressed and eat. We got a lot of work to do." I obeyed, but one glance out the window told me we wouldn't work outside. A line of black clouds darkened the west, and even as the east grew rosy with the sun, I heard thunder.

After breakfast, I found Pa out on the porch. He spoke as I came out. "The rain did damage in the attic and upstairs. Let's work on that." So we spent the day sanding and repainting in the bedrooms.

That night I took a long hot soak in the bathtub to remove all the paint I'd spilled. The water relaxed me until I closed my eyes and fell asleep. I woke in a panic, jumping up to get my head above the water, then slipping and falling with a crash onto the floor. I lay coughing. Too exhausted to make it down the stairs, I wrapped a towel around me and slept there.

The next morning, I heard Pa on the roof. I pulled on my clothes and went outside. He was tearing off old shingles, and when he saw me, he yelled, "Make a pile of the old stuff, over next to the woods." He pointed at a large patch of ground already littered with old shingles, tarpaper, and chunks of rotten wood.

I began to carry and pile what he'd stripped, and I'd barely made a dent when he yelled, "I need the big piece of plywood and the saw." I ran to obey, and he came down to measure and cut the plywood patch. Then he carried it up to nail in place.

He patched several holes before lunchtime, but he didn't stop long enough to eat. Instead he covered the entire roof with tarpaper. By the time he finished, it was dusk. I'd piled all the trash next to the woods and made supper for us both, but he took no notice. I admired Pa—he was a tireless worker—but nothing I did would ever please him.

At dawn the next morning, I found Pa on the ladder carrying bundles of shingles to the roof. Since there wasn't much I could do to help, I found a grassy spot and watched. I wondered if his job in the mine was this tiring. And then he did a night shift? How did he survive, year after year? It seemed to me that Jake lived better in his shed.

Pa took a break for breakfast and I joined him. "I need you up top now," he said. I scrambled up the ladder and gaped at the view. From the top of our house, you could see most of the valley, rolling green fields divided by trees lines, until you got to Walnut Springs. Beyond the town rose the foothills, and the Cumberlands stretched all the way into Kentucky. At least it was a pretty place to work.

Pa showed me how to cut the shingles straight, but the giant shears were too heavy for my hands. He cut while I nailed. Pa was real fussy that the shingles line up straight, and he checked each one before I nailed it down. When we finished the edge, he showed me how the next row overlapped. Before long, we both were nailing shingles, and the roof was changing color right before my eyes.

We finished almost half the roof that afternoon. By the end of the next day, we were done. I walked around the house picking up old nails while Pa nailed the last few shingles to the ridge. We did it! I would have danced for joy, but I was so tired that I almost couldn't eat. I passed out on my bed with all my clothes on.

The next morning, Pa shook me awake before dawn. "We gotta finish paintin' and move the furniture upstairs." When I groaned, he glared. "What d'you expect, we're on a picnic?"

I dragged myself upright and followed him upstairs. He was putting tape alongside all the trim. "White paint," he said, "and be real careful not to drip." I grabbed a brush and started to paint fast. "No!" he yelled. "You gotta go slow, all in one direction, like this."

I was happy to go slow, but it took all morning to paint the doors and doorways, window frames, and floor trim. By the time we finished, I could barely hold the brush. The afternoon promised to be sweltering. Already my shirt was sticking to my back, but Pa didn't slow a lick.

"Time to put the rugs down," he said, "and don't let 'em touch the paint."

My feet dragged as we lugged the rolls of carpet up the stairs. Luckily there were only four, and they rolled out fast. Now the bedrooms looked all neat and clean, but I felt like Pa had mopped the floors with me. And we still had furniture to move.

By late afternoon, the room started spinning and my vision kept blurring into grey. I'd carried my end of mattresses and bed-frames, then drawers full of clothes, all the dressers, and at the last, large piles of clothes and sheets and blankets for the closets.

Pa never stopped to rest, and if I stopped, he'd glare at me. If that didn't work, he'd yell, "Get your lazy ass movin' *now!*" And I moved.

We were done, or so I fervently hoped, but Pa couldn't seem to stop. "Clean the kitchen," he ordered. "Sweep the floors." I tried my best to obey him, but my body reached a point where it simply couldn't move. I collapsed on the sofa and lay still, eyes closed.

Ouch! The slap nearly knocked me off the couch. Pa pulled me upright by the back of my collar. I gasped for air as he glared down at me, his face contorted in a mask of pure hate. "You little punk. What d'you think your life is for? You think you're gonna gad around town on stolen money? This is what it's all about: *work*. If you ain't got it in you, you're a worthless piece of *shit*. Now start…"

I couldn't make out his final words, and then his face went fuzzy as everything around me faded into black.

Chapter 9

I slept all the way back to Mount Juliet. When we got there, Aunt Kate and Sarah greeted us, and Mamaw served a big meal in our honor. I ate, but I didn't say a word.

Mamaw eyed me with concern as I put my dishes in the kitchen and went straight upstairs to bed. My body ached so many ways I wanted to leave it, but my heart ached even worse. I'd failed my pa.

The next day, the house was in a flurry of packing with everyone preparing for our move to Walnut Springs. Sarah took me aside. "How's it look? Is it bad?"

"Naw, it looks great. We fixed it up all pretty." And I was proud of that, in spite of my exhaustion and Pa's temper. I managed a smile. "You'll be surprised."

Mamaw caught me next. "Did he work you hard?"

I shrugged. Pa and I were the only men in our family, and that required a degree of loyalty. I figured Mamaw knew. She went back to her chores, but she pressed her lips together in a most determined way.

By the next morning, Pa had stuffed the car trunk with Mamaw and Sarah's bags and boxes full of clothes. The rest lay piled on the floor of the backseat where Sarah and I took our usual places. Mamaw rode shotgun next to Pa.

I still ached, inside and out, and I spent the first hour rereading *Superman*. I wished I could be as strong as him. Then I stared out the window at the forest, and eventually my thoughts turned to Jake. I wanted to talk with him, tell him about Pa. Maybe he'd know what I did wrong. I tried to imagine what he'd say but couldn't. Instead I remembered what he'd told me at the train yard. He'd hoped that Ma and Pa would get our family back together, but if that didn't work out, I could find him. I grabbed hold of that promise and hung on.

We moved home on Saturday and school started Tuesday. Pa left early Sunday to see Ma, and since I wasn't up yet, Mamaw and Sarah went on to church without me. After breakfast, I reached underneath my bed and dragged out my secret stash of *Superman* comics. Mamaw and Sarah left me alone when they returned, and I was halfway through the stack when Pa got home. He banged in the front door, pounded up the stairs, and burst into my room. He grabbed the comic from my hands and glared. "Who gave you this?'

"Ma."

"D'you understand it?"

"Sure."

"What's it about?"

I began to tell the story, but he cut me off. "You read as good as anyone, and you can figure problems in your head. I ain't puttin' up with no more failin' grades just 'cause you're too *lazy* to do work. You understand?"

He leaned over me, his eyes narrowed into slits, and his eyebrows furrowed so close they were touching. I barely managed a nod.

"*You understand me?*" he repeated.

"Yes, sir," I squeaked.

"If you fail *anythin'*—a test, a quiz, your homework—you are *grounded* for the entire *year!*"

With that, he turned on his heel and marched out. I sat motionless, struggling to grasp the real-life meaning of his words. I would try my best, but I could see my future. Within a week I'd be a prisoner, unable to visit Lee, go fishing, or reach Harriman to have a talk with Jake. I was doomed.

When I didn't show for supper, Mamaw came to my room. She closed the door and sat down next to me. "What's wrong?"

I shrugged and focused on the walls. There was a pattern that the brush bristles made which caught my eye. I could lose myself in searching for the strokes.

"Pete." She spoke more forcefully. "Don't let your pa scare you. He treats us all like recruits in the Marines."

I read her face. She seemed sincere, but nothing she said made any difference. "He hates me."

"No, he doesn't hate you. He simply doesn't understand. All he knows about is life in the Marines, how to take and shout out orders. Don't look at me like that. I've known him longer than you've even been alive, and he behaves the same with everyone."

That should have made me feel a little better, but it didn't. "I'm gonna fail school again."

"Nonsense. You know everything; how could you fail?" Mamaw smiled.

I went back to studying the paint. No one believed me, but I knew I couldn't do it. I saw it written on the wall.

Tuesday came too quickly. The school bus stopped, and I climbed up the steps to join a rowdy group of kids. I looked around and saw Lee near the back, so I walked over and sat near him.

"Hi," I said.

"Welcome back, stranger." Lee had a wide grin on his face. "You got a lot of explainin' to do."

That was the truth, and I didn't even know where to begin.

"Why'd you run away?" he asked.

I looked down. There were so many reasons it was hard to say. But this was Lee, so I tried to make a list. "Ma was in the hospital, Pa was busy workin', I felt bad…" That sounded lame, even to my ears.

Lee raised his eyebrows, and I began again. "I flunked school."

Lee's eyes popped wide open. "You what?"

"I flunked. I have to repeat the whole fourth grade."

Lee looked puzzled, same as Jake and Pa. "How could you flunk?"

I shrugged.

"So you won't be in my classroom?"

"Yeah." My eyes focused on floor.

"Damn!" Lee said. "What did your pa say?"

"He told me if I fail anythin', a test or quiz or homework assignment, he'll ground me for the entire *year*."

Lee squinted his eyes, thinking hard. "You can do it. Just do everything the teacher says." He stayed silent for a moment. "I sure wish you were gonna be with me."

I should have looked at him, told him I would miss him. But the mean voice inside me said, *Don't make friends. They'll just get you into trouble.*

We rode in silence after that. When Lee stood up, he turned to me and said, "Good luck."

I didn't answer. I waited for all the other kids to leave and snuck inside the school and into the fourth-grade room.

And there she stood, Miss Clausen, my teacher from last year. Until I saw her, I hadn't even thought about the teacher. For some reason, I'd expected someone new. Miss Clausen's face showed no such surprise. She merely nodded as I pushed past all the little kids and sat at my old desk in the back.

That day recapped all my previous school failures. I tried to understand her, but I couldn't make heads or tails of anything she said. Luckily we didn't have homework, so I'd not failed— yet. As soon as I got home, I grabbed a fishing pole and took off like a bullet for the creek. I stayed there until my stomach started growling so loud it scared off all the fish.

I brought home two big catfish. Pa accepted my contribution to the freezer without comment. "Go wash up," he said. With supper already underway, Sarah was telling them all about her classes. In high school, she had a different teacher for each subject. I envied that. After she fell quiet, Mamaw turned to me.

"So how was your first day?"

I shrugged, but Pa glared. "I got Miss Clausen again," I mumbled.

"Well, what about the kids? Were they friendly?" Mamaw asked.

I rolled my eyes and stuffed my mouth with food. While I chewed, no one asked me stupid questions. Then Pa said, "What d'you learn today?"

"Nothin' much—it was the first day."

He frowned. "Got any homework?"

"Nope."

His frown deepened. "Did you bring home any books?"

"We can't. They stay in our desks at school." He already knew that, so I frowned at him.

"Don't try that shit with me!" He raised his voice; Sarah and Mamaw shrank back in their chairs.

I wiped the frown from my face and answered, "Yes, sir."

Pa scowled at me before starting on his food. We finished our meal in total silence.

The second day of school, I saw Lee outside at recess.

"How's it goin'?" he asked.

I shrugged. But his face looked different, and I studied him close up. His right eye had almost swollen shut. Furious, I asked, "Who gave you that?"

Lee looked down. He'd always been the smallest boy in our classroom, probably because his father was Chinese. Sometimes the bullyboys tried to pick on him, but in the past I'd always been there. Then I remembered his comment on the bus…

"Come on, Lee. Tell me!"

"Ricky."

"That big stupid oaf?" My eyes scanned the busy playground, and I spotted the culprit on the far side, playing football.

"No, Pete, don't! Your pa will kill you!" Lee grabbed at me, but too late.

I took off running, so angry I couldn't even think. I grabbed Ricky by the collar and tripped him. He fell on his face and scrambled to get up. I slugged him in the nose with all my strength. He yelped and grabbed his nose as blood spurted down his face.

I couldn't stop. I battered and bloodied his face with both my hands as fast and as hard as I could hit. He started screaming. The principal ran out and grabbed me, but it took him and two teachers to pull me off the kid. They led Ricky to the nurse and me to the office. From there, the principal called Pa.

I knew this meant bad trouble. Pa arrived, his face twisted with rage, hands clenched in fists, and muscles bulging underneath his shirt. He dragged me to the car and threw me in the back like a dog he couldn't wait to kill. He didn't even speak 'til we reached home. Mamaw came outside, her lips pursed so tight they'd disappeared. Pa dragged me to the barn.

"Pull your pants down," he ordered. I obeyed with shaking hands.

"Put both hands on the wall."

I stood trembling, my hands braced against the rough oak boards, my feet trapped in my pants. Pa reached for a long, thin, bamboo switch and started whipping like to kill me. I tried not to scream but the whip cut my butt and back and legs sharp as a knife. I clenched my teeth but still shrieked with every cut. My hands slid down the wall, and I'd curled into a ball when Mamaw came running.

"*Stop it,* Rob." she yelled. "Stop it or I'll call the *cops.*"

Pa threw in a bunch more licks before he quit.

"Go up to the bathroom," Mamaw said. I obeyed. Once safe behind a locked door, I wiped the tears from my face and tried to wipe the blood from my wounds. But it just stained the towels and kept on flowing. After a few minutes, Mamaw knocked.

"It's me," she said. I unlocked the door. She walked in with her hands full of medical supplies. "Take off your clothes." I pulled off the bloodstained remains.

"Get in the tub." Mamaw ran lukewarm water on my back. I shuddered and winced as it stung inside the cuts and ran red down the drain. She studied each slice in my flesh. "I think you can manage without stitches, but I'll have to use iodine. This will sting,"

I bit my lip, and then she set my back afire. Tears sprang into my eyes, but this time I didn't scream. Mamaw closed the deepest cuts with tape before winding a couple rolls of gauze around my body. I looked like a mummy when she finished.

"Now go to your room and lie on your stomach."

I retreated to my room. At first I felt so angry and sorry for myself, I couldn't even think about anybody else. But after an hour or more of cussing Pa, I knew that I'd deserved every lick. Most likely, I'd broken Ricky's nose, and his face would look a mess for weeks to come. I sincerely hoped that I'd not hurt his eyes or broke his teeth.

What was I thinking? It felt as if somebody inside me just took over. Then I heard the angry voice inside my head—*laughing*. That nasty part of me had grown stronger and stronger until I'd completely lost control.

I was a monster.

When I realized that truth, I knew I couldn't stay. I'd probably be suspended from school, and I couldn't trust myself around my friends or family. I'd become what Aunt Kate had always predicted, a violent criminal. I had no choice but to run.

Chapter 10

The school board put me on indefinite suspension, and while my back healed, I made plans. I began to gather things I'd need, like an old fishing pole, my jacket, my jackknife, Pa's old canteen, and a change of underclothes. I hid them out behind the barn. My comic book and flag were inside my pocket when Pa whipped me, and Mamaw most likely threw them out. No matter—I didn't even want them. Later I overheard Mamaw on the phone asking questions about a school for boys. Time was up.

My career as a criminal would begin with stealing. I hated that, but I didn't want to starve. I stayed up in my room 'til I heard Mamaw snoring. Then I snuck into her bedroom and took two dollars from her purse. In the kitchen, I filled up Pa's canteen, grabbed a loaf of bread, a couple cans of Spam, an apple, and a brand new box of cookies. I stuffed the money deep into my pocket. Last, I took a blanket and slipped out behind the barn. In the dark, I wrapped all my stuff inside the blanket and tied it with fishing line to the fishing pole. With the pole across my shoulders, I took off.

When I stepped from our driveway out onto the road, the night breeze blew cool and a sliver of moon rose in a clear starry sky. I followed our road out to the highway. The countryside slept, the roads deserted, and I managed to walk a long distance undisturbed. But I'd not slept a wink, and a little before sunrise, my eyelids started closing on their own. I looked around.

A short ways down the highway, I could see an old barn, weathered gray and leaning like a tree about to fall. I reached my goal shortly after sunrise and just before the traffic grew busy. I picked my way around an old barbwire fence, pushed through the overgrown weeds, and walked inside.

Except for the rusted pieces of an ancient plow, the barn floor appeared deserted. And the loft didn't hold a thing, not even hay. I climbed up there, spread out my blanket on the boards, and fell asleep.

Hours later, I woke with bright sunshine in my eyes. I stood, stretched, and stared out the window. The rolling hayfield below me covered a quarter mile square, the cut grass already turning brown. Beyond the field, a modern farmhouse stood beside a newer barn. I felt safe. I ate a slice of bread, my only apple, and drank half the water I'd brought in Pa's canteen. Satisfied, I climbed down and started out the door.

I froze. A rough-dressed man stood staring at the road, his back to me. I ducked inside the nearest stall just as he spun around and headed toward the barn. I heard another set of footsteps, and they stopped right outside the stall.

A raspy voice said, "What ya got?"

"Horse."

"How much?"

"Five for an ounce."

"I'll take twenty."

"Why? Ya sellin'?"

"Not your business."

"This *is* my business."

A gunshot blasted in my ear. I bit off a scream and strained to hear their footsteps disappearing. I crouched, trembling, as the silence closed around me. Finally, I peeked around the stall. I saw a black man...*hole* in his *face*...blood and brains splattered *everywhere*...

I bolted out the door and down the road, running faster and farther than I ever ran before. I didn't worry about cars or even cops. I didn't even stop 'til I got near Harriman. The sun was setting, and the evening breeze felt chilly when I leaned against a tree to catch my breath. I doubted that anyone had followed me that far. But a movement caught my eye—a man hiding in the shadows. He scared me so bad I took off again. I didn't stop until I reached the dump.

"Jake!" I gasped as I topped the rise. "Jake, it's Pete! I'm here."

There was no response, so I looked inside. Everything was there, just as before, and I didn't think Jake would leave his stuff unprotected. He'd be back. Afraid to light the lantern, I sat on his bed, all my attention focused on the darkness for a footstep, a gunshot, another person's breathing. I jumped when a dog barked, but no other sounds made it to my ears.

My breathing gradually slowed, but the muscles in my legs still trembled with exhaustion. It seemed like hours before they finally stopped. Then I made myself a sandwich and drank all the water left in the canteen. As I ate, I thought about the two men in the barn. I'd definitely heard a gunshot. But I didn't know for certain if the dead man was real or just a dream.

I found Jake's sleeping bag, laid it on the floor, and crawled inside. Eventually exhaustion won out over fear, and I slept sporadically, my nightmare waking me at early dawn. I got up. Jake's bed wasn't even rumpled, so wherever he'd gone, he'd stayed the night.

I began my day following Jake's routine. After a quick breakfast, I ran up to the spring pump to wash myself and refill the canteen. Then I walked up to the barn—maybe Jake slept there in winter. I climbed into the hayloft, and the blackest man I'd ever seen waved a greeting. I stared hard at him—he looked a lot like the dead man—but he was very much alive.

"Can I help you?" he asked.

"Well, maybe. I was lookin' for Jake."

He nodded. "Yeah, he's been gone since two weeks back."

"Oh." It took me a minute to process what he said. "Jake's gone? You know where?"

"The VA Hospital in Nashville."

"Is he sick?"

"I guess. I just got the job after he left. Maybe Mrs. Stevens can help. She's at the house."

"Thanks."

I climbed down and headed for the farmhouse. I feared Mrs. Stevens might ask why I was out of school, and I made up excuses in my mind before I knocked.

A small, gray-haired lady opened up. "Hello?"

"I'm lookin' for Jake, and the guy in the barn said he was sick. Can you tell me what happened?"

She studied me carefully. "Are you family?"

I nodded. It made a better story than anything I had.

"Well, then you probably know Jake has a drinkin' problem. He started drinkin' heavily a few weeks back, then got so sick we took him to the ER, and they sent him off to the VA."

Jake was a drunk? I tried to keep the shock from showing on my face. He never drank anything but water around me. Except once…He started drinking heavy when I left? Was I at fault? Was Jake another victim of my criminal tendencies? I stared at Mrs. Stevens a little bit too long. She closed the door.

My feet took me straight back to the shed where I sat on Jake's bed and tried to process all the facts. Drinking did explain why he lived here, but it didn't explain my experiences with him. And nothing he'd said about his history or his travels suggested he stayed drunk most of the time. It made no sense.

At least I knew where he was and how to get there. I only needed five dollars for the train, and while I worked out a plan, I could stay here. I moved the sleeping bag back to his bed and began to check out his supplies.

I knew I shouldn't snoop around Jake's shed, but once I got to checking out the food cans on the shelves, I discovered they contained a lot of things, but no food. A couple held bullets for the rifle, a few larger cans hid half-empty whiskey bottles, one held pens and paper, and the last two were stuffed full of cash. I faced a strong temptation to borrow, at least enough to buy a one-way passage on the train. But I put it all back exactly as he'd left it and made myself go outside and think.

Then I argued with myself. The bad news—Jake had nothing to eat. The good news—he had money. But Jake was my friend, and I didn't want to steal, not from him. I'd probably made him sick in the first place, and now I planned to take what little he had left?

I grabbed my fishing pole and walked up to the pond, then climbed the rocks and hiked along the creek. When I reached the spot where we'd fished before, I dug for a worm, but it was too late in the year. I found a half-dead spider, tied it to my hook, and tried to play the line the way Jake showed me. The fish didn't act the least bit interested, and after an hour without a single bite, neither was I.

By the time I reached the shed, I felt hopeless. Nothing was going like I planned. I lay on Jake's bed and worried about him, and Lee, and Ricky, and Ma, and Pa, and everybody else I might have hurt. I added Mamaw and Sarah to that list, especially since I stole their food and money. What else could I do?

I considered all my choices. If I went home, I'd probably be sent off to some military school. That would cost Pa money, and I'd never see Jake. But if I went to Nashville and told him all the things I'd done wrong, maybe he could help me. I needed *someone* to tell me why I beat up poor Ricky. Maybe Jake could figure out a solution to my mess, one that allowed me to undo all my sins and get back on the good side of my folks.

With a pang of conscience, I went back into Jake's hoard and counted out five one-dollar bills. I pulled out the two I stole from Mamaw but decided to keep those separate, for food. I knew the train I'd taken left at five, and there might be another train to Nashville leaving sooner. I packed up all my stuff and hiked to town.

As I walked, the angry voice grumbled in my head. *Jake's gone. You won't find him. And even if you do, he won't see you. You're the reason he got sick. Just kill yourself, you coward. Find a gun, put it to your head, and splatter your brains...* I struggled to regain control of my mind. I was worse than criminal—I was *nuts*.

Chapter 11

I already knew the train routine, but I didn't have Jake with me. I hoped Harper would remember. Most likely he rode the same train every day, and that meant I had to wait 'til five. But after a half-hour, when a long train rumbled in, I walked along the track to the caboose.

A tall, broad-shouldered man jumped off the back platform. He wore a railroad uniform, and from the rear he looked like Harper. I called out his name. But when he turned around, I saw an unknown man with a gun holstered at his hip. As he drew near, he reminded me of one of the gunmen in my dream. I turned and ran.

I sprinted toward the road, same as before. Somebody shouted, and I ran even faster. Then the ground started shaking, and the roar of an approaching train deafened my ears. A fully loaded coal train barreled down the track in front of me. I froze, close enough to reach out and touch it. My heart skipped several beats before I turned around and saw the bad man headed straight for me.

I took off alongside the speeding train, towards the back, and prayed it wasn't very long. The man began running and started gaining ground. I put everything I had into a final burst of speed and threw myself across the track, right behind the train. When I reached the road, I kept on running.

Before I'd gone too far, I looked back at the tracks. The man had disappeared, and as I watched, his train pulled out. I stopped, too shaky to run farther. I sat by the road and tried to pull my mind together. Was I dreaming again? Did he plan to kill or save me? I didn't know the answers, and now more than ever, I needed to find Jake.

But how? If I couldn't trust anyone, I couldn't get to Nashville. Bad men might work on trains, or drive trucks, or see me walking. Just like when I'd seen the black man in the barn, I didn't know if this was a nightmare or real. It took several minutes before I caught my breath and my mind calmed down enough to think. I decided to wait for the five p.m. train and prayed I'd find Harper aboard.

I spied a grassy spot on the far side of the road. From there I could watch the train yard and everybody in it, or run away if need be. Every little while, I snuck close enough to check the station clock. As the hours dragged by, I became convinced the grass in Tennessee grew faster than those hands moved.

The train arrived a little before five. It had the same mix of coal and boxcars as before. Still, it took all my courage to walk past them to the back. I didn't see Harper, so I climbed up on the rear platform and waited.

The train started moving before anyone appeared. Then a strange man leaped aboard. He wore the standard uniform, no gun, and he stared at me with shocked surprise.

"I'm Pete." I said. "Here's your money." I handed him Jake's one-dollar bills.

"You done this before?" The man gaped at me, but he took the money from my hand.

"About a month ago I made the trip with Harper. I'm a friend of Jake's." He narrowed his eyes and shook his head, so I knew both names were unfamiliar.

"Where ya headed?"

"Nashville."

"Big town. Anywhere in particular?"

"The VA Hospital."

A flash of recognition crossed his face. "That's good—we go about a mile from the place. But we might still be rollin' pretty fast. Can you jump?"

I shrugged. I didn't know exactly what he meant, and the idea of jumping from a fast moving train seemed both scary and exciting.

"Guess we'll see when we get there." He stretched out for a nap.

I sat and watched the countryside flash past. Atop the plateau, the trees were turning colors, and they made a picture postcard against the deep blue sky. I couldn't watch the sunset while looking to the east, but a few rays of pink reflected from the clouds about the time we passed, very slowly, through Mount Juliet.

The man hopped off. When he returned, I asked, "Can you tell me *exactly* when to jump?" He nodded.

I couldn't see any landmarks in the dark and prayed the route looked more familiar to him. About twenty minutes later, I felt the train slow down. The man squinted past the lights.

"Get ready," he said. I moved to the steps. "Jump!"

I threw my body out into the dark, hit a rocky slope and rolled 'til I stopped. Cautiously I wiggled all my parts, and except for a couple cuts and bruises here and there, everything worked fine. I stumbled to my feet, dusted off, and then realized I'd left my fishing pole and blanket on the train. Even if he'd thrown them, I'd never find them in the dark. At least I still had Mamaw's money.

I scrambled from the ditch and hiked toward a bright light off in the distance. Before long the light revealed a busy filling station, and as I reached the parking lot, I could see cars speeding on a highway. Once inside, I drooled over wrapped turkey sandwiches stacked neatly in a cooler, but their prices were insane. I could wait. A girl behind the counter asked if she could help.

"You know the way to the VA Hospital?"

"Of course. It's up White Bridge, over there." She pointed past the highway, and I saw another road heading north.

"How far?"

"About a mile, but you better hurry. I think their visiting hours end at nine."

I glanced at the clock behind her head. It read eight-thirty; I could make it. I approached the door just as a burly man pushed his way inside, and when he brushed past me, I felt something hard underneath his shirt. I turned to check him out, and he moved fast to grab me. I ducked and bolted quicker than a squirrel. I didn't look back. I didn't even stop for traffic on the highway. Had he recognized my face, or had he planned to rob and kill somebody there?

The voice inside my head gloated as I ran. *You'll never get away. You're too small, too slow, and much too stupid to escape. Stop running—let him catch you—end this misery right now.*

A streetlight in the parking lot ahead caught my eye. It lit a group of buildings spread out like a maze behind an inviting covered porch. The sign said Thayer VA Hospital. I flew up the steps and burst through the front doors, right into the arms of two guards wearing *guns*. The nearest one grabbed me. I stared up at him, my eyes bugging out and mouth ajar.

He said, "No kids allowed."

"Please…it's Jake…gotta see him…I *gotta*…don't *kill* me…*please!*" I pleaded between gasps for air.

A small gray-haired nurse appeared behind the guards. She spoke quietly to them and then took me by the hand and led me into a private room. She closed the door.

"What's wrong, son?"

"I need to talk to *Jake*."

"What's his last name?"

I froze. I didn't know.

To my surprise, she didn't miss a beat. "When was he admitted?"

"Two weeks back."

"And where's he from?"

"Harriman."

"Is he a relative of yours?"

"Kinda."

She narrowed her eyes. "Why do you need to see him?"

I wanted to tell her that I'd run for miles, heard a gunshot, saw a dead man, almost ran into a train, and jumped from another, all while escaping from dangerous men with guns. But I didn't know how much of that was truth or if she'd believe me. Instead, I said, "It's life and *death!*"

She studied me a minute. "I'll see what I can do. Stay here."

I couldn't go anywhere—there were two men with *guns* outside the door. Once she left, I crossed my fingers and toes and prayed aloud to Jesus. I promised him I'd be a perfect boy. I'd remember my prayers every night, never steal again, never lie, never run away.

The mean voice in my head started laughing. *You're lyin' right now. You're a liar and a thief and a bully and a bad son. You're breakin' His Commandments right and left. Just kill yourself. And if you're too much of a pussy, grab one of those guns and the guards will do it for you.*

Luckily, the nurse came right back in. "I think I found your Jake. Can you describe him?"

"Big guy, lots of hair and a beard, kinda brown and grey mixed together. Real blue eyes, sunk deep, thick eyebrows, and he's missin' a few teeth."

She smiled. "Yes, that would be Jake McDowell. If you tell me your name, I'll let him know you're here, but he'll have to come out to the lobby. No kids are allowed beyond these doors."

I told her my name, and she left. Then I dropped my sane act and started arguing with the voice. *You want me dead? If I die, you die, right? You sure that's what you want?*

I didn't want to die. That's why I felt so terrified, why I ran from all those men with guns. Men with guns. *Men with guns.* They were in my *nightmare—a gun up to my head...* I didn't even realize I was screaming 'til the nurse came running in. "He's coming, Pete. Please, calm down."

I did manage to stop screaming, but I couldn't stop trembling. And inside my head something splintered like glass into wicked, jagged pieces that kept shrieking in my ears. I grabbed my ears 'til Jake arrived.

Seeing him gave me another shock. He wore a gown, his arm attached by a long rubber tube to a metal pole. They'd cut his hair and trimmed his beard real short. His skin looked wrinkled and hung loose on his arms. In fact the only features I recognized right off were his amazingly blue eyes.

Jake sank into a chair and nodded for the nurse to leave. Once she closed the door, he reached out his hand. I grabbed it and felt a little safer, but neither of us spoke 'til I stopped shaking.

"Guess things aren't going very well," he rumbled, his deep voice both familiar and soothing.

"I'm gonna *die*." I told him, looking straight into his eyes.

Jake raised an eyebrow and leaned back in the chair. "How would you die?"

"Get one of them to shoot me." I pointed to the door.

"Why would you do that?"

I hesitated. Up 'til now, no one knew I'd gone nuts, and if I told Jake, he might tell somebody else. On the other hand, I didn't want to die. "I'm *crazy*. There's a monster in my head that

92

wants me to shoot myself, or get someone to do it, and I keep seein' all these *men with guns!"* I nodded at the door and saw his eyebrows raise a notch. Did he think I was completely nuts?

"They triggered you," he said, more to himself than to me. "Where did you first see these 'men with guns'?"

"In my nightmare."

That raised his eyebrows farther. "Maybe you should tell me more about your nightmare."

That wasn't at all what I'd planned. I wanted to tell him about Ma not coming home, about the roof and Pa's anger, about school and Lee and beating up on Ricky. But I trusted Jake, so I obeyed.

"It starts good. I'm in a different place, listenin' to music, and Ma sings. But all these men come in. They're carryin' *guns*, and they start yellin' and *shootin'* and everyone is *screamin'*."

I felt cold steel beneath my chin...the taunting voice...his sweat...his fingers holding me upright by my hair...

"*Pete,* talk to me." Jake squeezed my hand real tight.

"They're gonna *kill* me! He has a *gun* up to my head! If I tell you, they'll hunt me down and *kill me!"* I couldn't stop crying and shaking and clinging to his hand.

"Easy, Pete." Jake grabbed my other hand. He looked straight into my eyes and spoke slowly in his deep, soft voice. "You're safe here. Those guards at the door? They don't want to kill you. They're the good guys, and they'll stop any bad guys who try to come inside. Understand?"

I nodded, my eyes locked on his.

"We've got a lot more talking to do, and I promise we'll get to it. But the VA locks down at nine p.m. Have you got a place to stay?"

I shook my head, and he frowned. "I need to discuss this with Mrs. Sotherby, the nurse you met earlier. Will you be okay if I leave—just for a minute?"

"You're comin' back—tonight?" I kept hold of both his hands.

"Yes."

"Okay." I let go.

Jake stood slowly, wrapped his gown around his shrunken body, and dragged his pole behind him as he went out the door. He left the door ajar so I could watch while he talked and argued with the nurse. After a few minutes, he came back.

"You can't stay here, but Mrs. Sotherby lives close, and she's agreed to take you to her place. You can stay there for the night, but you'll have to be on your very best behavior. No stealing, no running off, no scary stuff. Okay?"

"What if I dream?"

Jake smiled. "I'm pretty sure she can cope with that."

Chapter 12

Mrs. Sotherby lived about a mile down the road. She walked slowly to her car and didn't talk at all as she drove home. I was grateful, as both my mind and body were wore out.

"You want supper?" she asked, once we were safe in her apartment.

I collapsed in a chair at her kitchen table, my hands and elbows holding up my head. I couldn't think straight. I didn't remember eating on the train, and ever since then I'd been running for my life. Now I felt too tired to be hungry.

"I'll fix you a snack, and you can eat it when you're ready." She put a flowery teapot on the stove and made up two ham, cheese, and pickle sandwiches. Then she placed mine on a dainty plate painted with blue flowers. It looked so fragile I didn't dare touch it. Mrs. Sotherby set it on the table. The glass for the milk had flowers on it too, but it didn't look as fragile, and the milk smelled fresh out of the fridge.

I drank the milk, and as I sat at her table in the warmth, with no pressure to talk or do anything at all, my mind began to function. I looked over at the quiet nurse. She was short, round, and lightly wrinkled, with dark gray hair drawn back into a bun. Outside of her age, she didn't look the least bit like Mamaw, but for some reason, she reminded me of her. I felt a little safer than I had earlier, and my appetite returned with a vengeance. The sandwich quickly disappeared.

She smiled. "Would you like some pie?"

That grabbed my attention, and I finally found my manners. "Yes, thank you ma'am."

"It's been a long time since I had a son to cook for."

"Where's your son?"

Her smile disappeared, and just as abruptly I knew her story. "Sorry."

"Not your fault."

We both remained quiet as I finished up the pie—apple, one of my many favorites. "Thanks." I handed her the dish.

"You can sleep on the sofa. I'll get you a blanket and a pillow…" She stopped and eyed me with pursed lips. I looked down at my clothes; they were covered with dirt and soaked through with sweat and blood. "Would you like to take a shower?" she asked.

To my surprise, I answered, "Yes." Next I found myself inside a ladies bathroom with more flowers on the towels, white carpet on the floor, and the faint scent of lilacs in the air. I pulled off my sneakers and carefully piled my filthy clothes on the toilet seat. In the shower, I let the warm water run all over me. It still stung inside the worst cuts from Pa's whip, and I'd added a few new ones jumping from the train. I bit my lip and washed my wounds with soap.

I was toweling off when she knocked on the door and handed me a bigger towel. "Wrap up in this. If you'll give me your clothes, I'll wash them for you."

I wrapped the towel around my waist and reached for my clothes. When I turned around again, she stood staring. "Who beat you?"

"Pa." I meant to add, "I deserved every lick," but my tongue refused to say the words.

"Good Lord, child!" She took my clothes and slammed the door behind her.

I stared at the door, unsure if Mrs. Sotherby was angry with me or with Pa. But she returned in a minute with a medicine jar and gently doctored all my injuries. That night I slept well, my cuts soothed with salve and my body wrapped in a soft warm robe inside even softer sheets. No nightmares interfered with my rest or hers.

By the time I awoke, Mrs. Sotherby had washed and dried my clothes, even ironed my blue jeans and old t-shirt. We dressed, ate, and drove back to the VA. I didn't know how to thank her proper, so I just touched her arm and said, "Thanks." She smiled, so I thought she understood.

Jake came downstairs around ten. He was still attached to the metal pole, but this time he wore a pair of pants and a robe. He grinned when he saw me.

"Hey, Pete, you look better. Did everything go all right with Mrs. Sotherby?"

I smiled and nodded.

"Did she tell you she served as a nurse in World War I?"

I raised my eyebrows while shaking my head. "How'd she lose her son?"

"In the Pacific." Jake gave me a funny look, as if I'd surprised him. Then he changed the subject.

"You came an awfully long way just to find me, Pete. Why?"

My brain focused immediately on the men with guns. But I didn't know how to tell him that. "I guess…'cause I went crazy."

He raised an eyebrow, asking for more.

"I beat up another kid, real bad."

"Why?"

"He hit my friend."

"You hit him back?"

"Yeah. But I lost it, big time. Beat him to pulp. It took three adults to pull me off. After that, I felt real sorry, but then it was too late. Pa came, and he looked just as angry as I felt. So he whipped me—bad."

Jake furrowed his brow. "Mrs. Sotherby said you have scars. May I see?"

I turned my back to him, pulled up my shirt, and lowered my pants.

Jake didn't say anything at all for a minute. I couldn't see his face, but his voice was strained and tight. "Has your pa whipped you before?"

"No." I pulled up my pants and turned to face him. "He usually just slaps me when he's mad. But then I've never hurt a kid before."

Jake took a deep breath and stared at me in silence, the way he always did when he needed time to think. "Is your ma home?"

"No. She won't come home. Sarah went to visit, and Ma wouldn't even see her."

Jake sighed and nodded as if it all made sense. "Let's get some lunch."

He led me toward a big open room, the cafeteria. We each took a tray, and I reached for Mamaw's money. Jake shook his head. "This one's on me." His words reminded me I'd stole five dollars from him. I felt so guilty, I couldn't meet his eyes, but I let him pile food up on my tray. Jake took a bowl of soup and crackers for himself. Once he'd paid with a punch card, I picked up my meal and followed him into a quiet corner.

I couldn't keep talking without telling Jake the truth, but I needed to find my courage first. I stared at the food—a hamburger with bacon, cheese, a pickle, and ketchup. I ate it. The French fries went next, and then the Coke. In fact I cleaned off that tray before I said a single word. Jake watched me while he ate his soup.

The food helped, and I started to explain. "I went to your place first."

He nodded.

"I met a black guy workin' in the barn. He told me where you were."

"Probably Norris. He's a good man, a hero in the war."

My eyes widened. I'd never met a Negro soldier.

Jake grinned at my surprise. "In a war zone, the color of your skin doesn't count for much."

I nodded and went back to my story. "I stayed at your shed." I checked his face, and he was smiling. "I was lookin' for some food, but I found a can of cash instead."

He snorted. "The VA sends me money every month. Guess I didn't know where else to keep it."

"I took five dollars for the train." Now I'd said it. I peeked up at his face, but he seemed calm. "I know I did wrong, and I promise to pay you back, but I had to get here. I'm real sorry."

Jake shrugged. "Maybe I left it there for you, who knows."

I let out my breath. He didn't act mad, and it felt good to get another sin off my chest.

"Do you want to talk about your nightmare?" he asked.

I nodded, but nothing came to mind. We sat there in silence.

"Let's put our trays away and go back to the lobby," Jake suggested.

I picked up my tray and followed him, and before long we were sitting in the little private room where we'd sat the night before.

Jake leaned back in his chair. "In your dream, do you know where you are?"

I shrugged. "Some fancy hotel, or nightclub, or some such place."

"Have you ever been there before?"

That made me think. Ma liked to sing for other folks, and over a year ago, she made plans to sing with a jazz group in Memphis. Pa approved it, and she took me with her. Strange that I'd *forgot* the whole thing.

"Yeah, in Memphis, the summer before last. Ma went to sing at a jazz club there. This looks pretty much the same."

Jake nodded. "Okay, you're at the club, and your ma's singing. Who else is there?"

"The pianist, he's black, and there's all the customers who came to hear her sing. It was packed. But the *men...*"

"*Whoa*," Jake interrupted me with a raised hand. "Let's just set the scene before they enter."

I stared at him, wide-eyed. He was treating my dream like a play, or a movie you could stop and run backwards. But I couldn't reverse the growing terror in my mind.

Jake continued speaking in his low, quiet voice. "How did you feel *before* the men came?"

"Happy. I love to hear Ma sing. And maybe I was sleepy, comfy in the chair. It felt soft...velvety." And for some strange reason, remembering that silly chair calmed me. I took a deep breath and stretched my shoulders.

Jake smiled as he watched. "And the other people, were they happy too?"

I nodded. "They were chattin' and laughin' and havin' a good time."

"So no one expected the armed men?"

I shook my head.

"Okay, now describe them."

"They wore uniforms."

"What kind of uniforms?"

"Khaki, but no Army stuff on them."

"So no insignia or patches?"

"No, nothin' at all."

"Anything else unusual about them? What about the guns?"

"Lots of guns. They all carried rifles in their hands, pistols at their sides, and plenty of ammo in their belts—and knives."

"Did they say anything?"

That question spooked me. My throat tightened 'til I couldn't speak.

Jake reached out his hand, and I took hold. "You're doing great, Pete. Just tell me what they said."

I squeezed his hand and took deep breaths before I even tried to talk. "The leader's the only one who spoke. First he swung his gun around, and guns were goin' off all over. Then he said, "Everybody get out—now!""

"Did they leave?"

"Most did. There were people screamin' and pushin' and runnin' every which way. But when I looked for Ma, she was lyin' on the floor. I sat by her."

"What about the pianist?"

I shuddered and covered my eyes, then my ears. I couldn't even think about that part.

"I guess he was still there?"

I nodded.

"What happened to him?"

I shook my head. I couldn't say it, and I didn't want to see it. But I did, every ugly, disgusting, bloody bit.

"No one's going to shoot you if you tell me." Jake spoke so soft I almost didn't hear him. "No one but you and me will ever know."

That made sense, so I tried my best to tell him. I really did. But I couldn't get the words out, and my head felt like it might explode. I started crying.

"It's okay, Pete." Jake reached over and squeezed both my hands. "You don't have to tell me everything today. We've got time."

Chapter 13

I spent another night with Mrs. Sotherby. She showed me pictures of her son growing up, and in the last one he wore a Marine uniform, much like Pa's. That made me smile, and I said, "He's real handsome." She smiled too, a sad sort of smile. Then she deep fried some chicken and served it with green salad and a baked potato drowned in melted cheese.

That night I dreamed, but this time my nightmare didn't start at the beginning. The men rushed in and grabbed the pianist. Ma tried to stop them, and they knocked her to the floor. When the pianist screamed, I screamed.

"*Pete*, wake up." Mrs. Sotherby's hand was on my shoulder. "You're safe. It's just a dream."

I shook myself awake, but then I actually remembered. As the whole ugly scene flashed through my brain, I realized it couldn't be a dream. "No, it's Memphis, and they *killed* him." I spoke before I thought, and then I stared at her in terror.

"Our secret," she said calmly. "Do you want another snack?"

I shook my head, too terrified to speak.

"I'll be in the bedroom. You try to get some sleep." She tucked me in and left the room, but I still tossed and turned 'til dawn.

When we arrived at the hospital that morning, Jake was up chatting with the guards. He wore his work clothes and had lost his metal pole. As soon as he saw me, he grinned wide, and then he went to talk with Mrs. Sotherby. When he returned, his expression had turned serious, and he motioned me to join him in our room.

"Mrs. Sotherby said you had a nightmare."

"Yeah, and I remember it."

He cocked his head. "What do you remember?"

"That it's real. I remember the pianist, how they held him down and...*hurt*...him."

Jake stared at my hands. I followed his eyes and saw that I'd made fists. He looked up at my face. "And then what happened?"

"They *shot* him."

Jake's eyes narrowed. "Did he die?"

I nodded. Jake waited for me to tell him more. When I stayed quiet he asked, "What happened next?"

This was the part I dreaded most. I'd not said a word when someone yelled out in the lobby, and the door to our room flew open wide. Jake jumped to his feet, and I prayed to disappear.

"*Pete*, get over here. We're goin' home *right now*."

Jake stepped in front of me just as Pa lunged. Faster than a blink, the two guards grabbed his arms and held him in place, one on each side. Pa froze, glaring through glazed eyes. He looked so crazy I doubted he even knew my name.

"Is this your pa?" Jake asked, eyebrows raised.

"Yes, sir," I automatically replied. Jake smiled wryly at the title, but then he turned to Pa.

"Mr. Martin, my name is Jake McDowell, and I'm Pete's friend. He came all the way to Nashville just to find me. And we've been talking, right here in this room. Pete spent his last two nights with Mrs. Sotherby, a trusted nurse. I promise you he's here by his own choice, and he's well cared for."

Pa continued to glare in my direction, face sweating, muscles bulging. The guards tightened their grip and braced their legs for a fight. I didn't want to be there if Pa chose to take them down, but Jake kept on talking as if Pa could understand.

"Pete's been telling me about his trip to Memphis, with his ma, the summer past. And I think there are parts of his story you don't know. Would you like to listen in?"

Pa's face softened, losing its angry stare, and his eyes refocused on my face. "You know what happened?"

The guards relaxed their grip, and Jake motioned to a chair. Pa perched on the front edge of his seat. I stayed behind Jake, as far from Pa as I could get. Jake turned to me. "You want to tell your pa what you told me?"

I shook my head.

"May I?"

I met his eyes, begging him for help. Jake seemed to understand and told Pa all about the men coming in, grabbing the pianist, and knocking Ma to the floor. Then he turned to me. "Can you tell us what happened next?"

I glanced from him to Pa and back at Jake. Pa waited, tense as a cat about to pounce. Jake appeared relaxed, so I tried to calm myself—it took a minute. Jake met my eyes with his supportive gaze, and I felt a little safer.

"When the men pushed Ma, she fell down and didn't move. I feared she was dead—'til she breathed. So I stayed…and they killed him."

"The pianist," Jake explained to Pa. "Tell your pa how they killed him."

I hesitated—there was more to this story, but his death might be enough. "They shot him." Jake already knew that, and he raised an eyebrow. I added, "In the *head*. It was *ugly.*"

Pa and Jake frowned and nodded in unison, and their calm reaction to such a violent death felt reassuring. Maybe you got used to all that stuff once you were grown.

Jake raised an eyebrow, and I kept my eyes glued on his. "After he died, the leader turned to Ma."

Jake nodded. "What'd he do?"

"He told his men to grab me. They dragged me to a chair, and this big ugly guy held onto me. I wanted to help Ma. *I tried to help.*"

My voice went all squeaky, and I felt like puking. If I said one more word, I would. I needed Jake's help, but he'd focused his attention on my pa. A look of horror had frozen on Pa's face, and he'd tensed his body for a fight.

"Mr. Martin." Jake's voice stayed very quiet. "Maybe we should take a break. Pete looks a little shaky."

Pa bellowed, jumping up and grabbing me. Jake had him by the throat and the guards had Pa in handcuffs before I really knew what happened. The guards pushed Pa into a chair, and he started screaming words he would have slapped me twice for saying.

"Oh my *God*. The bastards *raped* her. Fuckin' *perverts*. I warn't even there. She never *told* me. Oh my *God*." He continued his rant, but gradually, like a clock winding down, his speech grew slower and softer 'til it stopped.

"He had a shock," Jake told the guards. "Give him time."

I stared open-mouthed at Jake, unable to understand why he took Pa's side. But Jake sat down right next to Pa and waited. Pa took a deep breath, and another. When he turned and saw Jake, a flash of anger crossed his face. Then he dropped his head and sighed.

"Better?" Jake spoke real soft and gentle, like he did to me when I was spooked.

Pa nodded, and Jake asked the guards to release him.

"I know that had to come as quite a shock," Jake said to Pa. "But sometimes you need to know the truth."

Pa nodded again, although his eyebrows remained pinched, his fists clenched. I kept puzzling on why he'd lost control, with no success.

"I think we all need a break," Jake said. "I know a pretty place not too far from here where we can walk, or sit, and just relax. I've been stuck in this joint for two weeks now, and this is the first day I'm off the IV. So if you're okay with it, I'd like to get outside."

"I'll go along," Pa said, relief softening his face.

Jake turned to me, one eyebrow raised in question.

I felt scared, and he knew it. But I had to trust someone, and anyone who managed to best Pa got my respect.

"Okay." My eyes warned Jake to keep me safe.

We set out, Jake walking beside Pa and me trailing a little bit behind. Jake started off by telling Pa how we met, but then he said something that grabbed my full attention.

"I had a wife and son once," Jake told Pa. "I worked as a mechanic—mostly serviced diesel engines on the freighters. We traveled all around the world. But when our ship needed a complete overhaul, we headed for the docks at Rotterdam, in Holland. That's where I first saw her, waiting table. Her name was Matilda, and she moved like a dancer with a graceful beauty that made other people smile. I fell hard and took a job at the docks so I could stay. In three months we married, and nine months later our son, Adam, arrived. That was in 1938."

Pa raised an eyebrow. "What happened when the German's came?"

"My wife was part German, so she felt fairly safe behind their lines. Of course life got tough—little food, unfair rules—but I stayed with my family until we learned about Pearl Harbor. Then I left."

"How?"

Jake looked down, his forehead wrinkled deep. "I hid on a freighter, jumped ship when we docked to refuel in North Africa, and worked my way back from there to England."

Pa nodded, his face just as grim. When Jake told it, you didn't feel the fear or see the danger, but Pa had experience behind enemy lines. "Then you enlisted?"

"Yeah. Most of our Navy headed out for the Pacific, and I wanted to be near my wife and son. So I joined the Army, worked on tanks, until they needed me to drive."

Jake stopped and pointed to a peaceful park, a lush green meadow that stretched downhill to the river. Plenty of big oaks stood scattered through the green, their rusty leaves drifting to the ground.

Jake headed for a wooden bench nearby. "Still haven't got my strength back," he admitted as he shakily lowered his body to the bench. Pa sat beside him, and I stayed on the grass, behind Jake.

"What happened to your family?" Pa asked.

Jake sighed. "Things got so rough in Holland that Matilda took Adam to her family in Berlin. I'd visited her folks before the war, so I was okay with her living in Berlin. Until it fell into Russian hands. It took me weeks to get their papers straightened out. Then I needed permission just to cross the Russian line."

Jake paused and Pa's eyebrows rose. "What happened?"

"They were gone. I asked the neighbors, and they said that sometime before Christmas the Nazis grabbed her father. Shortly after that, the family fled."

"You couldn't find them?"

"I found out where they went." Jake didn't say a word for several minutes, and I couldn't see his face. When he spoke again, his voice sounded hoarse. "They went to Dresden."

"Not *Dresden.*" Pa emphasized the word as if the name alone contained an explanation.

Jake remained so quiet that I walked around to see his face. He'd hidden it behind his hands, but silent tears dripped between his fingers. Neither he nor Pa said a word. I didn't know anything to say, so I busied myself digging for worms.

When Jake sniffed loudly, I looked up. He wiped his face and shook his head. Once he'd recovered, he turned and spoke to Pa. "Pete told me your wife's been in the hospital for months, and he told me how hard you've worked to keep your family going. But no matter how difficult it gets, at least you still *have* your wife and kids."

Pa nodded, and his eyes appeared misty, but maybe I just imagined it.

Jake squinted up at the sky. "It must be lunchtime. I need to go back and take my pills. Pete?" I ran over to the bench. Pa frowned at my dirty hands, but Jake managed a weak smile. "Ready to go back?"

We walked very slowly since Jake looked wore out. Once we reached the VA, he spoke to the guards and then to Pa. "I need a break. You and Pete are welcome to stay here. You can leave anytime you want, but Pete has to go willingly. If you try to force him, the guards will intervene."

Pa's face tightened in anger, but Jake pinned him with a blue-eyed stare. Much to my surprise, Pa backed down.

"The cafeteria is right down that hall." Jake pointed the way, and then he left.

I stood there with Pa. We stared at one another as if we were meeting for the very first time and neither one of us knew what to say. Finally he asked, "Are you hungry?"

"Yeah."

After we washed up, I led the way into the cafeteria, and Pa bought us dinner. I opted for another hamburger and fries. He followed suit. Then he chose the table, like always, and moved his chair to face the door, its back against a solid wall.

"How's Ma?" I asked.

"About the same. She may have to come home since I can't pay the bills. But if I don't find a job soon, there won't be no home for her to come to."

"You lost your *job*?"

"I took too many days off between weekends to see your ma, two weeks to fix the roof, and then huntin' everywhere for you."

"I'm sorry." I bit my lip and stared down at the floor.

He sighed. "It warn't just you—mostly it's your ma. She's been so sick, and I wanted her to have the best of care. That's what pushed our family, and me, right to the edge. But she never told me 'bout Memphis. And after what you said, it's clear that's when all the trouble started."

We ate in silence, this time a peaceful silence. I carefully ran through Jake's story in my mind, but I still didn't understand. I asked Pa, "What happened to Jake's family? Did they die?"

Pa narrowed his eyes at me. "Eavesdroppin'?"

I flinched at his accusing tone.

He stared at me a minute and then dropped his eyes. "You'll hear 'bout it anyway. The Germans were bombin' the British up in London, 'most every night. They burnt a lot of buildin's and killed a lot of innocent civilians. So the British and our Air Force launched a counter attack. We firebombed Dresden. And when we finished, there warn't nothin' left but ash."

"*We* killed Jake's family?" I couldn't believe it.

"Yeah."

Chapter 14

Pa and I were still talking when Jake reappeared. He walked within earshot just as I asked Pa, "How do you plan to find a job?"

Pa glared—he'd not meant for me to tell. But when Jake sat down beside him and unfolded a newspaper, Pa turned to him and said, "I told Pete I lost my job. Now I guess he's worryin' 'bout how I'll pay the bills. He don't need to worry. I'll find work—I always do."

Jake nodded and rubbed his neatly trimmed beard. Then he put aside the paper. "Have you looked at the government plants in Oak Ridge? They're pretty close to Walnut Springs."

Pa shook his head. "They hire scientists and engineers and such."

"Sure," Jake said, "and those guys need support. So they also hire craftsmen, janitors, and, above all, security guards for all their nuclear supplies. I'd think someone with your military background might fit right in over there."

"Why, thanks." Pa looked more hopeful.

Jake shared his newspaper with Pa. I didn't have much interest in the news, but since both of them were reading, I glanced at the headline: "Gang Violence Escalates in Memphis." That caught my attention. I tried to read more, but Pa and Jake exchanged a worried glance.

"You sure you want to read this?" Jake asked.

"Does it tell about me and Ma?"

"No, it's about some recent shootin's," Pa explained. "It says, 'several eyewitnesses have described the criminals.'" If they catch the men, would you wanna see their pictures? See if you recognize their faces?"

"No." My stomach cramped.

"If the pictures went public, they'd never know," Pa said.

I shook my head vigorously.

Jake flashed me a smile. "They don't have any suspects, Pete, much less any pictures. You don't have to worry about it now."

He meant to reassure me, but it failed. I hadn't expected the law to get involved. And the longer I thought on it, the more it filled my brain. Would I have to go to court and tell everyone what happened? If I talked, I knew the men would kill me. And they might kill Ma and Pa and Sarah too.

I turned to Jake. He was studying my face, sneaking in my head like only he could do. "What's the matter, Pete? You worried about something?"

I nodded.

"You want to talk to me, your pa, or both of us together?"

I really wanted to speak with Jake alone, but Pa would ask me to repeat it all for him. "Both," I said. Pa's face relaxed.

We retreated to our room off the lobby and took the same seats we'd had earlier that day. We'd barely sat when I asked,

"If they arrest the men, will I have to talk in front of *them*?" Just saying the words made me feel sick.

Pa answered. "You're still a kid, Pete, so you don't have to testify, but it might help convict 'em if you did. And that'd make a huge difference to your ma."

I stared at Jake, and he returned my gaze with real concern. "You okay?"

I shook my head and put my hand over my mouth.

Jake found an empty wastebasket and handed it to me. "Are you scared he'll kill you?"

I closed my mouth, pulled my knees up to my chest, and wrapped my arms around them, saying nothing.

"One of the men put a gun to Pete's head and threatened to kill him," Jake explained.

Pa's eyes widened, but then he switched to his military face. "Don't be scairt. You know I won't let nobody hurt you." While I watched his face and listened to his words, I could almost believe that Pa was Superman, and for a brief moment, I felt safe.

Jake stayed quiet, studying Pa. When he turned back to me, his face grew more concerned. "Would it help you to talk about the men?"

I lifted my head and met his eyes. There was one memory I could *not* escape. It kept repeating and repeating… Maybe Jake could make it go away. I locked my eyes on his as I spoke. "The man they killed, the black piano guy?"

Both men nodded.

"They hurt him, real bad. I was with Ma, but he screamed

so loud I had to look. They bent his fingers...'til they *broke... one by one.*" My hands curled into fists, and my eyes closed as tight, but inside my head I still heard him screaming, *Not my fingers! That's my job, my livin'. Break my legs, not my fingers!*

I shook my head to stop the screams, and when that didn't work, I yelled at Jake, "I keep *hearin'* him, and *seein'* him, and I can't make it *stop!*"

"Easy, Pete. You're safe here." Jake wrapped his hands around my fists. I opened my eyes and saw his eyes were fixed on Pa. Then I saw why. Pa's face was twisted with some strong emotion, and as he slowly clenched his fists, I feared he'd hit me. But he spoke instead, his voice hoarse and strained.

"The man who did that is evil, a devil. He enjoys hurtin' people and makin' people scream. *He should be shot!*"

Pa scared me so bad, I prayed the guards were near. Then the nasty voice inside my head started mocking him. *Should we shoot Pa? Did he enjoy whippin' us and makin' us scream?* I wanted to hit myself to get rid of that voice. I wanted to run away from *me.*

Jake met my desperate stare with total understanding. "Hang in there," he whispered as he squeezed my hands in his. My eyes clung to him, trusting he'd protect me. But when he spoke, it was to Pa.

"Mr. Martin, it sounds like you're speaking from experience. Is that true?"

Pa's hands shook so hard he braced his fists against his head. I heard him moan.

"Do you want to share what happened?"

Pa shook his head. His breathing raced and his eyes leaked tears. I knew he was hurting bad, although I had no idea why.

"That's okay. Just remember you're still in Tennessee, with your son, you're safe, and you're *home*." Jake continued talking very gently, calming Pa with his voice and leading him back from someplace dangerous and painful. I watched as Pa stopped trembling and his muscles relaxed. He finally sighed and opened up his hands.

"Better?" Jake asked, and Pa nodded.

Jake waited until Pa raised his head and met his eyes. "I know how that feels— I've been there. What little I know, I learned from my doctor. If you need someone to talk with, Dr. Brown is right here at the VA."

It seemed a reasonable suggestion, but Pa firmly shook his head.

Jake sighed and turned to me. "What your pa said is true— some men are evil. But sometimes good people get pushed beyond their limits, and then they act just as cruel."

Pa dropped his eyes again, and no one said a word until he spoke. "Jake's right, but that don't excuse me for beatin' you that day. I'm real sorry, Pete. I don't know why I did it."

Shocked, I nearly forgave Pa on the spot. He never apologized to nobody for nothing. But I couldn't let it go. I never knew when he'd explode, so it would be a lie told out of fear.

Jake waited for me to answer Pa. When the silence grew uncomfortable, he asked, "Are you ready to tell us what happened to your ma?"

I'd been avoiding that. And with Pa so upset, it made things even worse. "Do I have to? Now?" I asked Jake.

"No, you don't have to talk at all. But I promise that *nobody* will hurt you. And *no one* will make you testify."

Jake narrowed his eyes at Pa. Pa sighed real deep and turned to me. "Pete, I promise to keep you safe, not hurt you, and not force you to speak in court." Then he raised an eyebrow. "But I'd like to know everythin' that happened, if you feel up to tellin' me."

I didn't want to say a word. Of all the ugly things I saw that night, what they did to my mother was the most difficult to tell. But now I owed Pa since he both apologized and promised. After a deep, shaky breath, I began.

"The big ugly guy held onto me…the leader tore off her pretty clothes…Ma woke up…started fightin'…screamin'… two other men grabbed her…held her down…"

I was too embarrassed to look at Pa or Jake. Then I remembered what Jake told me. He'd said, "It's always okay to tell the truth." That helped.

"The leader…he lay on top of her…kept *hurtin'* her…I *tried to help*…" I felt too sick to continue. My nightmare spun ahead, out of control. About to puke and too terrified to cry, I closed my eyes and curled up tight, struggling just to hold myself together…big ugly guy…gun beneath my chin…*gunshots… screams…*

I started shaking, and Jake squeezed my hands. Pa said, "Let me," and Jake released his hold. Pa wrapped both his arms around my body. He smelled of sweat and soap, familiar and safe, and when he pulled me tight against his chest, I started sobbing.

"I'm sorry Pa...couldn't help her...wanted to...couldn't... *I failed...please, forgive me!"*

"Shhhh," Pa soothed me. "You ain't got nothin' to be sorry for, Pete. You did fine. A grown man couldn't of done better. And bad as it was, you both survived. So you did good."

I couldn't believe what I heard. Pa wasn't mad at me? He said I did *good*? I felt such relief, such surprise, that I cried even harder. Pa still held me.

After a while, I glanced up and realized Pa was crying too. Even Jake was chewing on his lip, but when he saw my eyes, he whispered, "Good job."

Pa let me go, and I used my shirt to wipe my face. He did the same with his.

"Pete, I need to tell you somethin'."

Pa's calm voice reassured me, so I listened.

"I thought all this year you were runnin' from the truth, from your failure at school, from hard work. But I got it backwards— it was *me*. I was hidin' from the truth of what happened to your ma, and you were just tryin' to understand. I'm sorry, son. You didn't fail us; I failed you both."

Then he spoke to Jake. "I really want to thank you for helpin' Pete and me. If there's ever anythin' I can do to help you, let me know—I'm in your debt. But now, with your permission, may I please take my son home?"

Jake turned to me. "Are you okay with that? Is there anything else you need to tell me?"

My head was in a terrible muddle. There was so much more that I wanted to tell Jake, things I could only say to him. But I felt good with Pa—he wasn't angry. The only big problem I could see with going home would be school.

"Pa, what happens when I'm home? Are you plannin' to send me off?"

Pa met my eyes, his face real serious. "You made some bad decisions, son. You know that, and now I understand better why you did. But I'll have to talk with Mamaw 'bout your school."

I studied his face. In spite of his serious look, I saw a gentler smile in Pa's eyes. I trusted that.

Chapter 15

On the long drive home, I thought about Pa and his reactions to my memory. I still didn't understand why he'd lost control, especially when I told him about Ma. He said "the bastards *raped* her." I didn't know the word, but I guessed it meant a special kind of hurt, like what the leader did.

Pa went crazy when I told about the pianist. I hated that part too, but the super- nasty demons in Pa's head hurt him *terrible*. Jake knew how to tame them, and I needed to learn how, 'cause they'd frightened the bejesus out of me.

I needed more time to talk with Jake. I'd not asked him about the dead man in the barn, or the men carrying guns at the train yard and filling station. I still didn't know if they were really after me. There was more to my memory as well. But if I didn't think on it, maybe it would just fade away.

One thing stood out for a fact; I'd *never* be strong enough to fight off five armed men. Strangely, that didn't make me sad. Instead it freed me from an awful guilty feeling that had hung above my head ever since the trip to Memphis. Pa said I did good, that a grown man couldn't have done better. Which meant all the evil things the bad men did that night were *not my fault*.

With a huge sigh of relief, I gave up on my secret dream of being Superman.

Soon as I got home, I gathered up my whole collection of *Superman* comics, even the pictures I'd pinned on my wall, and took them to the cleared area out back. I placed a few charred logs around the pile and lit the corners with a match. Mamaw saw them burning and started to complain, but Pa told her to let me be. I watched while the pages transformed into smoke and 'til only a small heap of ash remained. That reminded me of Jake's lost family, so I asked Lord Jesus to be extra kind to them, and while He was at it, to help Jake.

Mamaw told Pa she would school me at home. I'd forgotten that she used to be a teacher. Pa told me I'd need to finish all my homework and never leave home without asking him or Mamaw, or else they'd send me off as planned. I agreed.

Pa went out every day to look for work. He received one offer from the Co-op, but I could tell from his face that it wouldn't be his first choice. A few days later, he kept grinning all through supper. Finally, when I couldn't wait a minute more to ask, he said, "I got a job. It's at the Y-12 plant in Oak Ridge. They do top secret military stuff, and they were hirin' guards. So I signed on."

That news made me smile ear to ear. I wanted to thank Jake and tried to call him, but our phone line was dead. I planned to write him a letter, but before I even started, Pa took me aside and told me Ma would be coming home next week. Then I couldn't concentrate on *nothing*. What had Pa told her? Had I made her mad by telling? If Pa hadn't told her, should I?

Since my mind refused to focus, I struggled with schoolwork. Faced with a history test, I camped out in the kitchen and tried to memorize a list of dates and names. But I'd been rereading the same list for an hour when the school bus squealed to a stop. Outside the window, Sarah waved at Mamaw, who was hanging up laundry in the yard.

Sarah barged through the front door and straight into the kitchen. Her face flushed with anger, she demanded, "What's goin' on? You run away from home after Pa stripes your back. Now *that* I understand. But then he quits his job just to find you, and you two come back here like best buddies? Even Mamaw treats you special and agrees to teach you school. That makes no sense at all. You need to explain what really happened."

I knew how she felt. When adults kept secrets, it always drove me crazy. That's why I learned to eavesdrop. But I couldn't tell her everything. You can't just dump that kind of stuff on your friends, or even your big sister. And what should I tell her about Jake?

"Well?" she said. "Don't look so confused. It can't be that hard to tell the truth."

About telling the truth, she definitely was wrong. But I picked through the facts and decided what she needed. "You remember when Ma and I went to Memphis last year?"

"Yeah?"

"Well somethin' happened. I didn't wanna think about it, Ma didn't tell, and Pa and you and Mamaw didn't know. But I guess you got a right to know, 'specially since Ma's comin' home on Sunday."

Sarah squirmed with curiosity.

I took a deep breath and stared down at my books. My throat tightened. I could never explain what I saw happening to Ma, but maybe I could say the word Pa used. "One night in early August, while we were in Memphis, some men broke into the nightclub where she sang." My voice grew so hoarse I had to whisper. "They *raped* her."

Sarah's eyes grew wide. "Oh my God!" she said, a hand raised to her mouth. "No wonder she didn't tell anyone, not even Pa. Does that mean the baby wasn't his?"

Her question caught me by surprise. I tilted my head and met her eyes, questioning.

Sarah put on her know-it-all expression. "It takes nine months to grow a baby; Ma told me that when she was pregnant." Together we counted out the months and stared at one another, mouths ajar. My baby brother, the little blue creature in Pa's shoebox, the one we buried with our prayers and flowers underneath the redbud tree, had never been Pa's son.

"Did he know?" Sarah asked.

I puzzled on that question. "Well, he could do the math, same as us. He musta known, but he clearly didn't know about the rape."

"So what would he have thought?"

The answer was obvious—and ugly. "He musta thought Ma was a tramp."

Sarah nodded. "That could explain why he went to Kentucky."

"And why they never talked."

"Yeah. Wow!" Sarah wrinkled up her face. "That's an awful secret. How did you find out? Were you there?"

I turned back to my books. "I got a test."

Sarah hesitated, but then she left the room.

Sunday arrived. Mamaw insisted we all go to church, so we did. I worried the entire time over Ma's return and never heard a word the preacher said. I paid little more attention to the snow covered fields and the cold bite in the morning air. Once home, Mamaw started cooking and cleaning, and Sarah helped her in the kitchen. I stayed in my room, pacing and worrying about what to say to Ma, what not to say, and wondering what she'd say to me.

Still pacing, by this time in the parlor, I watched through the window as Ma and Pa arrived. Ma seemed frail. But even with her long blond hair pulled into a ponytail and her slender body bundled in a coat, she looked more beautiful than ever. Pa held her hand as she slowly climbed the porch steps, and then he went back to get her bags. Mamaw met her at the door. They hugged and kissed while Sarah and I waited, she by the kitchen door and I by the parlor.

Ma turned to Sarah first. She didn't say a thing—just stood there and stroked her daughter's face. Sarah looked frozen, as though she didn't know what else to do. Finally Ma said, "You grew up. I left a little girl and came back to a young woman." Then Ma burst into tears, and without a word to me, she fled upstairs.

"She's tired from the trip," Mamaw said. "Come help me get dinner on the table."

We set the plates and silverware around. Pa came in, and Mamaw nodded toward the stairs. With bags in hand, he followed Ma. I wanted in the worst way to eavesdrop from the stairwell, and I could see Sarah strain her ears. But with Mamaw there, we couldn't learn a thing.

Pretty soon Pa came back down. He made a plate for Ma and went upstairs again. After a bit, he joined us at the table.

"She needs a little time to settle in," he said.

The conversation lagged, even when Mamaw talked about my schooling and how I'd not finished up my homework. Pa looked at me real serious, but I knew he didn't care, that he couldn't stop worrying about Ma.

The next couple days, Ma never spoke to me at all. She'd see me from across the room and turn the other way, or pass me in the hallway and hurry up the stairs. I couldn't figure out what I'd done wrong. She annoyed me so, I waited outside on the porch. As soon as Pa got home, I grabbed his arm.

"What's goin' on?" I asked. "Why is Ma avoidin' me? What did you tell her? Is she mad?"

He sighed real deep, and then he sat down on the porch steps. I settled right beside him. "Son, I've not told your ma nothin' 'bout Memphis. She ain't ready yet. She's so fragile and emotional and physically weak, it might be the death of her."

"You think she'd cut her wrists again?"

"Maybe, or take an overdose of that medicine she's on, or somethin' worse. I cain't take that chance." He met my eyes. His were dark with fear and filling up with tears. I knew better than to argue.

Mamaw coaxed Ma to come downstairs, sit out on the porch steps, help around the house. Ma would obey up to a point, but then she'd simply sit and stare. I even started taking things to her room: a book, a cup of tea, or food for her to eat. But she'd turn her face away and wait until I left. Then, I suspect, she went right back to staring.

This continued until Christmas, and the weather outside stayed just as bleak. Freezing rain covered all the branches with ice, and some got so heavy they fell across the road. Pa and I cut them up for firewood. Then it turned so bitter cold my breath froze in the air and solid ice covered all the roads.

In spite of the weather, we prepared for Christmas morning. We cut and decorated a fat cedar tree, and everybody made a special present for Ma. On Christmas morning, we lit a fire in the fireplace and waited and waited for her to come downstairs. She never did. I'd carved her a real pretty pin, so finally I took the box and ran up to her room.

When I opened the door, I saw a needle in her arm. "Is that your medicine?"

Ma almost dropped the needle. Then she said, "Yes." I gave her the pin, but she laid it on the bed without as much as a glance.

"Everybody's waitin' in the parlor."

Ma went back to staring at the walls.

"What d'you see there?"

Ma didn't answer, and in less than a minute she fell over on her side. I ran to the top of the stairs and yelled, "Mamaw. Come up here. Now!"

Mamaw flew up the stairs and checked Ma's pulse and breathing. "She's okay, Pete. That's just how the medicine affects her. She'll wake up in an hour."

"What's in it?"

Mamaw shrugged. "It's something she brought from Chattanooga."

"What's it s'posed to do, make her sleep?"

Mamaw shot me a puzzled look. "That's a darned good question." She went into the bathroom and put a pinch of the white powder in an empty aspirin bottle. "I'm going to ask the pharmacist."

Several days later, we all learned the truth. Ma was shooting heroin like an addict. Mamaw confronted Ma, went through her room, and threw away every single trace of white powder. Pa cussed out the doctors and the hospital and staff, and I stayed far away from him. Then Ma kept getting sick, vomiting and running to the bathroom all the time. She didn't eat a thing, barely drank water, and looked so pale and shaky that we all feared for her life.

I wrote to Jake.

Chapter 16

Pa also developed an addiction—to the news. He'd closely followed the violence in Memphis ever since Jake showed him the newspaper that day. The police called in suspects, but they told the cops that gangsters controlled them by threatening their families. The cops handed it over to the FBI, and that's when Pa started to nag me. He wanted me to "tell all" to the Feds, but I said, "No."

"It'd help your ma," Pa said.

"It'd get us killed."

"I won't let that happen."

"You're not even *here* most days."

"If I'd seen their faces, I'd talk."

And that's where our arguments dead-ended. He stayed brave and stupid, and I remained a coward. I couldn't get around that fact.

Then one afternoon, before Sarah came from school and while Mamaw was out shopping, the phone rang.

"Hello," I answered.

"Hi Pete. This is Mrs. Sotherby, the nurse at the VA Hospital in Nashville?"

I nearly dropped the phone. And as soon as we'd exchanged the polite formalities, I blurted out, "How's Jake?"

"That's why I called. I received your letter, but he left a month ago."

My heart sank. "Do you know where he is?"

"Not really. The only address we have is a post office box in Harriman. Would you like that?"

"No. If he's in Harriman, I'll find him. Thanks."

After she hung up, I started worrying. Why did she call me? Did Jake need our help? That shed must be well below freezing in this cold. I worried so much I went outside and waited in the frigid air for Pa. As soon as he turned into the driveway, I ran over.

"Can you take me to Harriman? *Please!* The hospital called, and I gotta check on Jake."

Pa stared at me a moment. "Get in."

Pa drove too fast, his fingers gripped the steering wheel too tight, and when we reached the dump, his foot stepped too hard on the brake. We skidded past the dirt road, but snow and ice had made the rutted slope impassable. I showed him where to park up by the farmhouse. Then I ran and slid down the snowy hillside, past the spring pump, and pushed aside a tarp hanging over the shed door.

Jake lay on his bed, curled up in his sleeping bag and covered up with blankets. His breath had frozen into ice on his beard, and his face was terribly pale. "Hey Pete," he rasped, his voice hoarse. "What a nice surprise."

"Pa brought me." Right on cue, Pa reached the door.

Jake pushed himself into a sitting position, legs still inside his sleeping bag. He wrapped the blankets tight around his shoulders. "Mr. Martin, please come in."

A mixture of emotions crossed Pa's face. He wrinkled up his nose at the makeshift shed and furrowed his brow, staring at Jake. Then his eyes darted all around the inside of the shed, taking stock of Jake's possessions.

"All I got is water, but it's fresh from the spring. Would you like some?" Jake asked.

I helped myself, but Pa shook his head.

"Pete wanted to check on you. It's been bitter cold."

"Warmer than Alaska." Jake tried to laugh, but instead he started hacking, real deep and nasty. When he poured himself some water, his hands shook.

Pa finished checking out the shed. "I see you got a stove. Do you have any propane?"

Jake stared at his trembling hands. "Haven't been to town. Cold as it's been, guess I better make the trip."

"I'll get your can refilled."

Jake reached for his money, but Pa shook his head. "I owe you for the Oak Ridge tip. I got a security job at Y-12 last fall, and now I'm in your debt twice over."

That brought a little smile to Jake's face. "Glad to hear it." He turned to where I was sitting on the floor. "How's school?"

I shrugged. "Mamaw's teachin' me at home, so it's some better."

"And your ma?"

Pa narrowed his eyes at me, but I ignored the warning. "She's home, but she's real sick, in withdrawals."

Jake looked at Pa, and Pa glared at me. But then he sighed. "She got some heroin, passed it off as medicine, and took it every day since she come home."

The corners of Jake's eyes and mouth drooped in sympathy. "How did you find out?"

"Her ma got suspicious and asked the pharmacist. When we learned the truth, I called the hospital doctor, and he said she was in withdrawals when she got there—back in *June*."

Pa hung his head, and I watched Jake. He rubbed his beard, which had almost grown back to its old length.

"Addictions are very hard to break. I should know. When I lost my wife and son, I started drinking. I drank so much it almost killed me."

Pa's eyebrows rose, but he kept listening.

"And even knowing that, I still drink. I don't know if that makes me more or less qualified to help, but the only way I know to stop using, is to stop."

"She's done that, but now she's really sick," I said.

Jake nodded. "Yeah. But after a couple weeks, those symptoms will improve. It's the craving that lasts…and the denial."

Jake coughed again and cleared his throat. I glanced at Pa. He'd perched on the far end of the bed, and now he held his face between clenched fists.

Jake followed my gaze, and his expression softened. "The medicine that helped me most is very inexpensive—truth. But sometimes it's difficult to take."

Pa lifted his head and met Jake's eyes. "I never told her. Not a word of what you and Pete told me. I thought it'd make her worse."

Jake snorted. "Yeah, everybody thinks that. My friends let me dodge the truth for years. That's why nothing changed 'til I got to the VA and the doctor there insisted that I tell him everything."

"But what if she tries to kill herself?" Pa unclenched his fists, his face pale.

"You need to be careful, make sure she can't get to a gun or lethal drugs. But beyond that, it's a chance you have to take." Jake's voice stayed firm, but his gentle eyes held Pa's, supporting him.

Pa took a deep breath and straightened his spine. "What should I tell her?"

"She knows what happened. What you really need to do is let her talk."

"But she *won't* talk!" I burst in.

"You need to show her that it's okay to talk. Make an example of yourself for a start. Then ask just enough questions to keep her story going. It's not easy. She'll be sad and angry, and she'll probably want to hit you at some point. But as far as I know, it's the only way."

Pa hung his head, studying the plywood floor. He chewed on his lip, deep in thought. After a bit, he looked at Jake. "Would you help?"

Jake's eyebrows rose abruptly. "What could I do?"

"Come back with us, talk to her. I think you have a talent that I'm not sure I have. And they'd be safer while I'm workin'."

"It's a long walk from here."

"You could stay; we got an extra room."

Jake sighed deep and wrinkled up his forehead.

I could see him struggling to make a good decision, and I really wanted him to come. "It'd be like last summer, but at my house."

Jake laughed, but that brought on another fit of coughing. When he could speak again, he said, "I have to say it's tempting, especially this winter. But there is...something else...you need to know." Jake covered his face, sighed deep, and then looked straight at Pa. "After the war, I spent a couple years in prison."

"What for?" Pa asked, though he didn't sound surprised.

Jake looked down and chewed his lip. Finally he admitted, "Manslaughter. I killed a man, a neighbor. But I didn't know what I was doing at the time."

"Were you drunk?" Pa asked, his voice disapproving.

"No." Jake shook his head. "That was before I started drinking."

In a flash, I understood what happened. "You had a waking dream, like last summer!"

Jake met my gaze and nodded. "The police said I was in a cemetery throwing gravestones all around. This guy grabbed me, and I picked up a stone and smashed his head." He looked down. "I thought I was in Belgium, after a terrible battle... turning over bodies...searching...for friends..." He covered his face with both hands.

Pa studied Jake, eyes sad, lips pursed. "Ever happen again?"

"No. My doctor doesn't think I'm violent now. But I still have that dream, and it scares me."

"You'd have your own room, and there's lots of space outside if you need to be alone. Would that help?" Pa asked.

Jake looked up. "Could you tell your family not to touch me if I act strange?"

Pa snorted. "Livin' with me, they already know that." Then he frowned at Jake. "We have rules too: no drinkin', smokin', gamblin', or women. If you gotta drink, you gotta leave, and don't come back home 'til you're sober. Can you live with that?"

Jake met Pa's stare. "I'll do my best."

Pa's face softened to a smile. "Get your stuff."

Chapter 17

W hen we turned into the driveway, I noticed Sarah on the porch. She jumped up as we exited the car.

"Where have y'all been? Mamaw and I already ate."

"Sorry," Pa said. "I didn't think it'd take so long. We brought a friend to stay with us awhile. This is Jake McDowell, and this is my daughter, Sarah Martin."

Jake bowed to Sarah. "It's a pleasure to meet such a beautiful young woman. I'm sorry we're late, but your pa insisted that I come."

Sarah blushed and ran into the house. We followed. Mamaw came from the kitchen and glared at Pa, but when she spotted Jake, she forced a smile. "Hello?"

"I'm Jake McDowell, a friend of Pete's." Jake reached out his hand.

Mamaw shook it. "Everybody here calls me Mamaw."

"Jake came to help us with Helga," Pa explained.

Mamaw eyed Jake more closely, and I could see he met with mixed reviews. She pursed her lips at his poor health and hygiene, but her face relaxed when she saw his gentle manners and heard his educated speech. Completing her appraisal, she rolled her eyes and waved him to the parlor with her usual "Make yourself at home." Then she hurried to the kitchen and began to warm up leftovers.

Over supper, Pa talked about the violence in Memphis. There'd been another shooting, and the FBI now offered a reward for any information that led to an arrest.

"We sure could use the money." Pa stared straight at me.

I made a marathon of chewing up my chicken.

"Has he seen the pictures?" Jake asked.

"No, he's refused. I promised I'd not make him testify, but he might, at the very least, identify their faces. That's not hard."

Pa sounded annoyed, not yet angry, although I could feel his anger building. He would never be satisfied until the FBI caught, tried, and hanged the man who injured Ma. My appetite abruptly disappeared. I turned to Jake.

"Why me? Why not ask her? She's the one he hurt. And she could see his face better than me."

"You're wife isn't eating?" Jake asked Pa.

"She ate earlier," Mamaw said.

"She never eats with us anyway," Sarah added with a pout.

Jake's eyebrows rose at Sarah's comment, but he quickly lowered them. "Pete told me she'd been sick. And he thought I could help her through withdrawals."

A heavy weight dropped from my shoulders. Jake had followed my lead and put the focus back on Ma. Maybe I could figure out a way to keep it there, 'cause whenever Pa went off on his FBI addiction, I wanted to run away again.

After supper, Mamaw fixed the attic guestroom while Jake took a long hot soak in the tub. Mamaw asked me to pick up his clothes for her to wash, and I knocked on the bathroom door. "It's Pete."

"Come in," Jake rumbled.

"Mamaw wants to wash your clothes, so I brought Pa's robe." I hadn't seen Jake naked since last summer. Then he was big and strong and tanned. Now, as he stood and wrapped himself in the robe, his bony ribs and sunken gut surprised me. Even so, Pa's robe looked like it'd shrunk several sizes as Jake tied the sash around his waist.

"How've you been?" Jake's voice was low and gentle. "Any nightmares?"

"Yeah." I focused on the floor.

"When your Pa brings up the FBI?"

"Yeah. Why is that?" I glanced up at his face.

"It's a trigger, like seeing the guards at the VA. All sorts of things can trigger a bad dream, or even a waking dream."

That caught my attention. "A wakin' dream, like you had?"

Jake nodded and eased himself down to the tub rim.

"Do you ever see things, like people who aren't really there?"

Jake raised an eyebrow, "Do you?"

"Once. When I was hikin' to your place the second time, I stopped to sleep at an old barn. Two men came inside, and they were arguin'. Then one of 'em shot off his gun, and they both ran. I was tryin' to sneak out when I saw the black man shot dead on the floor. But I ran across the floor where I saw him, and *nothin'*."

Jake nodded. "That's happened to me too. It even happened once when we were fishing."

My eyes widened.

"I saw someone running in the woods. I thought it might be you, so I followed. I was worried, thought you might be in trouble, and I guess that brought back memories of the war..." Jake rubbed his forehead and sighed before continuing. "Anyway, I came out in a field that was fresh plowed and saw dead bodies all around, everywhere. It scared me so bad I ran back to the pond and found some whiskey that I'd stashed..."

Jake bit his lip and hung his head. I couldn't tell if he felt embarrassed or just sick. Then I recalled his story about prison. "Were you afraid you'd hurt me?"

He lifted his head and met my eyes. "You bet I was."

"So did I start you drinkin'?"

He shook his head. "No, that was my choice—a stupid choice I admit—but not your fault."

Jake stood slowly and headed upstairs to his room. I followed. Once there, Jake unpacked a change of clothes. They weren't much cleaner than the ones he just took off, but he put them on for bed. When I didn't leave, he sat down and patted the mattress beside him. I bounced onto the bed.

"Still worried about the FBI?"

"Yeah."

"You know, your pa isn't trying to upset you. He thinks your ma would feel safer if those bad men were in jail."

"I almost puke every time he asks."

Jake grew thoughtful, staring into space. "I remember back in Europe I always felt like throwing up right before a battle, and some of the infantrymen threw up as they marched. But when it came to fighting, we fought as well as anybody there."

"They weren't cowards?"

He met my eyes. "Not at all. Bravery is overcoming fear, not lack of it. In lots of situations, especially at war, fear is the only reasonable response. But then you overcome it and do what you must."

I thought on that for a moment. "What if I can't do it?"

Jake just smiled, and I already knew that I could try.

"Get some sleep," he said.

I left, remembering to drop Jake's clothes into the laundry before I said my prayers and fell into bed.

The next morning, Pa introduced Jake to Ma. He'd already told her that we had a guest, so she was sitting up in bed—a gracious queen surrounded by a silk embroidered coverlet carefully arranged over her throne. Mamaw and Sarah were working in the kitchen. I snuck halfway up the stairs and crouched there, listening.

As soon as they finished the formal introductions, Ma asked Jake in a sugary- sweet voice, "How did you and Rob first meet?"

"Your husband came to the VA, looking for Pete. But when he got there, Pete and I were deep in conversation, so we invited him to stay and talk."

I thought Ma might ask him about our conversation, but she completely changed the subject.

"You speak like a Northerner. Where are you from?"

"Originally, Alaska. But I've traveled extensively, all around the world. You're also a Northerner—Wisconsin?"

"Duluth, Minnesota, but I've been right here in Tennessee for twenty years. Thought by now I'd have a southern accent." She smiled.

Jake didn't smile back. "I hear you're a singer. What type of music?"

Ma watched Jake with a puzzled stare. "Mostly jazz."

"Like Billie Holiday? She's one of my favorites."

Ma relaxed. "I sing 'Easy Living' and 'Lady Sings the Blues,' though no one can compete with her voice. Have you heard Ella Fitzgerald?"

Jake grinned. "Yeah, she was popular in Europe."

"I hear she's come out with a new album, Cole Porter songs," Ma said.

"I'd like to hear that."

At least she and Jake had found some common ground. They chatted about music until Jake began to cough, and then he excused himself. I wondered why he never asked anything important, but he didn't, and Pa said even less.

When Jake and Pa disappeared downstairs, I went by Ma's room and asked if she needed anything. As soon as she saw me, her face tensed, and she snarled, "Why'd you bring that man here? How'd *you* meet?"

"I ran away."

She narrowed her eyes at me. "Why?"

I remembered what Jake said about the truth. "I felt bad about what happened when you went to sing in Memphis."

Ma turned white, then red, and she screamed, "How *dare* you throw that in my face, you little *pervert*? Get *out* of my room. Get out *now!*"

I ran to the stairs as Jake and Pa came rushing up. Jake grabbed my shoulder and stopped me in my tracks.

Pa pushed past us to the bedroom. "What's the matter, Helga?"

"*He* felt bad about what happened back in Memphis? Well he's the one who caused it. If he weren't so much trouble, I'd have left him home with Mamaw. It's *his* fault. "

Jake squeezed my shoulder while Pa tried to reason with her. Ma glared and yelled, "Get him out of my sight. *Now!*"

Jake and I withdrew to my bedroom just as Mamaw stormed past us up the stairs. She yelled at Ma. "How dare you talk that way about your son. You have no idea what that boy's been through ever since you dragged him off to Memphis. You nearly got him *killed*. And if it weren't for our guest, he might not be here now. So shut your mouth and listen to your husband."

Ma jumped out of bed and ran into the bathroom, locking the door. Through the wall, I heard her hack and puke. I turned to Jake.

He sighed. "She'll get over that, unless she's feeling real upset."

After a bit, Ma returned to the bedroom. She turned her back on Mamaw and stayed close to Pa where he waited near the door. He started talking.

"Pete's been in trouble since you two returned from Memphis, and I never thought to ask him why. Like you, I made it all his fault. When he ran away the first time, I got real strict and grounded him. When he beat up that kid, I switched him hard. But when he ran away again, I quit my job and hunted everywhere to find him.

"He'd gone all the way to Nashville to see Jake. I walked in that hospital demandin' he come home. Instead they made me listen to everythin' that happened. It *hurt*, but I finally understood what you survived."

"Nothing happened there." Ma's voice was tight with anger.

"If nothin' happened, how come you got pregnant?"

Ma slapped his face so hard it made me wince. Pa caught her hands and held them. "You cain't deny you had a baby."

"Let go of me, you *brute*."

Pa released her hands. "Answer my question."

Ma attacked him again, this time with her fists. She hit him on the arms and chest, but Pa didn't even block her. He just took it, and eventually she broke down in tears. He put his arms around her, and she cuddled close.

I looked at Jake, and he nodded toward the door. We retreated downstairs to the kitchen. After a few minutes, Mamaw joined us. "I've never seen Helga that upset. Not even when I caught her stealing from my purse."

That comment raised both my eyebrows, but who was I to judge another thief.

"I think your pa handled that quite well," Jake said. "I guess he didn't need me."

"But I did."

Jake smiled and poured milk for us both.

About an hour later, Pa came down, looking tired but more hopeful. He nodded at me. "Your ma would like to talk to you."

I glanced at Jake, and he pushed himself slowly to his feet. The three of us walked upstairs together. I thought Ma would apologize, or at least talk nice, so I smiled as I walked into the room. But as soon as she saw me, her expression changed—her face tensed and she spoke between clenched teeth.

"I rue the day I ever birthed you. You've been nothing but trouble ever since. Your Pa did right to whip you—he should've *killed* you. I should've killed you before you were ever *born.* "

I shot out the door, down the stairs, and outside. Jake followed close behind. The afternoon was damp, cold, and gray, and the bare branches of the trees against the sky looked as dead as Ma's wishes for my future. I raced all the way to the creek, never slowing 'til I slipped and nearly fell on the ice. Jake caught me and put one arm around me while he coughed and I sobbed.

"She hates me. She wants me *dead*." I started to hit Jake, but he grabbed my hands and held them tight.

"When did she start that kind of talk?"

"Last year." I struggled to break free from his grip.

"And before that?"

I gave up fighting and thought back. "She used to sing and read books and throw me birthday parties." It was hard to believe that she was the same person. My old ma loved me, but this woman hated me. Was that any different from my beating up on Ricky? I wasn't my normal self then, either.

"He musta got inside her," I said.

Jake stared at me. "You mean the guy in Memphis?"

"Yeah. Kinda like the other guy got inside of me."

Jake stiffened and let go of my hands. I looked up in surprise as he studied me with a deeply worried expression. "How did the other guy get 'inside' you?"

I tried to find words, but instead I gagged. Luckily I hadn't eaten lately. Jake sighed and put his hand on my shoulder. "It's okay, Pete. I understand."

"He said he'd kill me and Ma if I *didn't*, and he had a gun up to my head. So I tried, but it made me puke all over."

Jake started to say something, but instead he coughed and hacked until beads of sweat ran down his face. He stepped away from me, wiping his forehead and scowling at the ice beneath his feet. I didn't understand. Was he sicker? Was he angry? Had I done something too disgusting to discuss?

Eventually he croaked, "What happened next?"

I glared up at Jake, too upset to tell him all the rest. Instead I told him the part he'd want to hear. "Another man came in, yelled somethin', and they left."

Jake wiped the sweat from his face and closed his eyes. Then he took a deep breath and focused hard on me. "I understand how that man got in your head, but I don't know how that feels."

"I told you!" I yelled. "He's there all the time. He makes fun of me, tells me to run, and he's always wantin' me to *die!*"

Jake puzzled for a bit. "You think the other man, the leader, is inside your ma's head the same way?"

I nodded vigorously. "He *hates* me. She's okay with Pa, or Sarah, even you. But when I come near her, he takes over. Then she treats me awful, wants me *dead*."

A light came on in Jake's blue eyes. "Of course, you trigger her."

He'd explained about triggers, but I didn't follow. "I make Ma crazy? Why?"

"Because you were there when she got hurt. Every time she sees you, it reminds her of what happened. Then she feels terrified, and angry, and acts crazy. *That's* what happened."

Jake sighed and smiled as if he'd solved his puzzle, but then he coughed so hard his body shook. Motioning me to follow, he shambled toward the house in between spasms of hard coughing. I trailed behind, expecting him to listen once we got there. But as soon as he opened the front door, Jake croaked, "Sorry." I watched as he stumbled up the two flights of stairs and firmly closed his door behind him.

I stood staring, angry as a hornet and now totally confused.

Chapter 18

That night Jake's coughing woke me, and on Sunday he coughed so much he didn't eat at all. On Monday, Mamaw stopped by the Co-op for some horse pills. She said they'd fix his cough, but Jake barely left his attic room for days.

I couldn't sleep, and I couldn't do my schoolwork. Mamaw reminded me, Pa threatened, but I was too upset to even care. On Thursday afternoon, while I sat in the kitchen staring blankly at my books, Jake came downstairs and made himself a pot of tea and toast.

He pulled up a chair right next to me. "What's going on?"

I scowled real ugly. "What do you care? You're here to fix Ma. Leave me alone."

Jake's eyes widened with surprise and hurt. I felt like shit and looked down at the floor. He finished eating and then touched my shoulder. "I think we need to talk; let's go outside."

The sun had reappeared that afternoon, so Jake and I settled on the porch steps. Jake still seemed shaky, and in spite of the sunshine, snow covered the fields as far as I could see. He motioned for me to slide a little closer and wrapped his big coat around us both.

"Let's go over everything you told me, but more slowly," he suggested.

So we did. Most of it was easier this time. Jake smiled, and I started to relax. Then he asked, "What did that man make you do?"

I dropped my head and wouldn't talk.

"Are you thinking you did something *wrong*?" Jake's deep voice soothed me, like warm tea. I glanced up.

Jake met my gaze, his eyes direct but gentle. "When there's a loaded gun pointed at your head, the usual rules don't apply. *Anything* you did that helped you and your ma live was *okay*."

The longer I thought on that, the more it made sense. It would have been okay to shoot the man. I sighed deep and added, "But I puked."

Jake shrugged. "So?"

I shook my head, annoyed with him again. "I didn't *mean* to."

"I know." Jake searched my face, his head cocked. "It stopped him from doing you more harm, didn't it?"

"No! He *shot* me!" As I said it, tears sprang to my eyes.

Jake's blue eyes opened wide. "Shot you? Where?"

"My ear—it was bleedin'."

"Which ear?"

"The right." I touched it lightly. Jake leaned over to take a closer peek, but I already knew it looked okay.

Jake let out his breath as he sat up. "I don't think the bullet hit you. Stare straight at me." He put a hand on either side of my face. "Don't turn your head; just tell me what you hear."

I pointed to the left. "You're squeakin' your fingers."

"And on the right?"

"Nothin'."

"Now turn your head to the right until you hear it."

I twisted my head all the way before I heard squeaking on the left.

"You're deaf on that side," he said. "Did he fire his gun right by your ear?"

"Yeah! It hurt."

"Just the noise from an explosion or a gunshot can do damage. That's what happened to my ears."

"In the tank?"

He dropped his gaze. "A grenade. One of my buddies took the worst..." Jake rubbed his fists against his forehead, and I watched him closely as he struggled with that memory. After a bit, he shook his head hard and went on.

"The blast knocked me down—hit my head, some shrapnel, nothing serious— except when I came around I couldn't hear a thing. The doctors fixed my right ear, but they couldn't do much for the left. That's why I always set you on my right, or if you're in front of me, I turn my head a little. Otherwise, I can't hear."

I thought about us talking in the shed. When he sat on the bed, I was always on his right. And when we talked at the VA, Jake stayed on my left. Then I thought back to when I couldn't hear.

"In Miss Clausen's class, I sat at the back, by the windows. I could kinda understand her if she stayed near the front. But she liked to walk up and down the aisles to my right, and then I couldn't figure out a thing."

Jake smiled and ruffled my hair. "Guess we solved that mystery. I knew you were much too smart to flunk."

That made me smile. Maybe I wasn't so stupid after all. But thinking about school reminded me of Ricky, and my smile quickly disappeared. "I *still* don't understand why I did it."

"Did what?"

"Beat up Ricky."

Jake pried into me with his sharp blue eyes. "What happens in your head when you're upset?"

I stared down at the steps and recalled the last few times. "I talk mean to Sarah, even Lee, when the man inside me says somethin' real insultin'. But when he tells me to kill myself, or Pa, then I get *crazy*...feels like my head is splittin' open. I'd *never* hurt *Pa!"*

"You'd hurt yourself?" Jake's forehead wrinkled with concern.

I thought on that and shook my head. "When it gets that bad, I run away."

"Does running help?"

I remembered the second time I ran and how terrified I felt about everything that happened. "Not really."

"What helps?"

"Talkin' to you. That's why I went to Nashville. I had to tell *someone*." I sought Jake's eyes for reassurance.

His gentle gaze held mine. "Yeah, I know. Talking helps me too." He was quiet for a bit before he asked, "Does your pa ever scare you?"

"Sometimes, when his voice gets too high, or he tenses all his muscles and looks crazy. That's when I really wanna run."

"Does he hit you?"

"He usually slaps me when he's mad, but not lately."

"How does that feel?"

"It *hurts*. And then I get all angry and upset." Just thinking about it made me so furious, I wanted to hit someone—hard.

Jake kept an eye on my clenched fists. "What else does he do that you don't like?"

"He orders me around. And when he works, he's a robot, never stops, never rests, and he expects me to do the same. Once, when we were workin' on the roof, he got so mad he picked me up by my collar and was yellin' in my face when I blacked out."

Jake tensed, but then he took a long, deep breath. "Were you upset with your pa when you went to school that day?"

I bit my lip and barely nodded.

"Did you want to hit him?"

My eyes bugged out, and I quickly shook my head. "I would *never*…"

"Too scary?" Jake held my gaze and raised an eyebrow.

My head bobbed vigorously.

Jake snorted. "Yeah, I wouldn't pick a fight with him either. But sometimes when you really want to do something and can't, you might do it to another person."

I puzzled on that one. "You think I beat up Ricky 'cause I wanted to hit Pa?"

Jake shrugged, so I knew it was a guess. But the more I thought, the more it made sense. Pa had dogged me hard after I first ran away. He'd hit me for my schoolwork, riding on the bus, the roof—and he'd threatened to ground me for a year.

"I *hated* him then."

"Are things any better?"

"Some. He's not on my case so bad, but he stays awful close to breakin'."

"Yeah." Jake rested his head against the railing. "Do you know what's troubling him?"

"No."

Jake shook his head once quickly, as if to let loose of that unanswered question. Then he gave my shoulders a quick squeeze. "You okay now?"

I smiled and leaned back against the porch steps. Jake sighed deep and did the same. We rested there in peaceful silence, watching as the sun slipped behind the foothills and the stars made their nightly appearance in the sky.

Chapter 19

Sunday night, I knocked on the door to Sarah's room. She'd just spent the weekend visiting Nancy, her best friend. As I peeked inside, she stood looking in the mirror. Her reflection scowled back at me.

"What d'you want?" she snapped.

"Did you see Lee?" Lee's family lived near Nancy, up the mountain on the other side of town.

Sarah sighed and dropped down on her bed. "You won't like it."

That piqued my interest, so I pushed my way inside and plopped down right beside her on the bed. "You saw him? Talked to him?"

"Of course. He asked all about you."

"What'd you say?"

Sarah pursed her lips. "I told him Pa whipped you, and you ran away—this time all the way to Nashville—and how Pa went after you. Then I told him about Ma, and Jake, and everythin' that's happened since."

I nodded, impressed that Lee had gotten her to talk. "What'd he say?"

"He wanted to see you, but we couldn't figure out a place and time. Pa'd whip you again if you skipped school."

"Can't he come over here?"

Sarah shook her head. "His pa won't let him—says our family is too violent."

That hurt. I'd been protecting Lee for years! I glared at Sarah, and when she met my eyes, I could see she understood. "Would he meet me somewhere in between?"

"We talked about the swimmin' hole."

I thought hard. It took an hour to hike there, an hour back, and we'd need a couple hours to make it worth the trip. I sighed, and Sarah dropped her gaze.

The next day, my mind was so preoccupied with Lee that Mamaw nearly slapped me for not listening to her teaching. After school, I went straight to Jake. He smiled when he saw me. "Hey, Pete. How's it going?"

I shook my head. "I got a problem."

His eyebrows rose. "Past or present?"

"It's Lee. He wants to see me, but his family won't bring him, Pa can't take me, and it takes too long to walk."

"You asked your pa?"

I shook my head. "*His* pa said our family is too violent."

Jake sighed. "Let me talk with your pa."

I waited a whole day, wiggling in my seat all through school. Afterwards, I bugged Jake again, and he said. "If you can arrange a time and place, *we* can go."

My eyes opened wide—I hadn't thought of that. Then I got Sarah to ask Nancy to ask Lee to meet me at the swimming hole Friday after school. I thought about phoning, but his ma might answer, and she'd probably ground him just for talking to me. It took two days to get a response, but I already knew Lee would come.

It rained all Friday morning. I'd never let the rain keep me home, but it was a cold rain, and I had to think of Jake. Luckily, the skies dried up by noon. We set out early and reached the swimming hole, an abandoned limestone quarry filled with water, around three. I'd heard rumors that it measured one hundred feet deep, but nobody really knew for sure. The steep edges were strewn with crushed rock and difficult to climb on a dry day, much less wet. Jake and I rested on a boulder near the top. He was tired and still coughing. I stayed close.

My eyes popped wide when I glimpsed Lee. He didn't come alone—he brought Ricky. I elbowed Jake, who was close to nodding off.

"Jake, wake up, it's Lee and *Ricky*."

Jake peered up the trail. Lee and Ricky stood together like best buddies, staring down at us. Then Lee led the way, but my eyes fixed on Ricky. To my great relief, the beating I gave him hadn't scarred his face.

Lee grinned when he got near. "Hey, Pete. I knew Jake was comin', so I thought you wouldn't mind if Ricky came. He apologized, and now we're friends."

I nodded at Ricky and squinted hard at Lee—he could at least have warned me. Then I said, "Glad you got here okay."

"Sarah told me you're doin' school at home."

"Yeah, fifth grade, same as you guys." My mind focused on Ricky; what should I say? I turned and met his worried eyes. "I'm real sorry I beat you. I was pissed at Pa and guess I took it out on you. Glad you healed okay."

Ricky frowned, studying my face. "They had to set my nose, and that hurt worse'n you breakin' it."

I looked closely at his nose. "It looks great—even better than before."

"That's what I told 'em." Ricky started to smile, but when he glanced down at my hands, his smile faded. I followed his gaze and realized I'd made fists. Taking a deep breath, I opened them.

Lee smiled. "Ricky's been watchin' out for me, with you gone…" He started to say more, but he stopped and glanced at Ricky.

Ricky looked down at the ground. "I been stayin' with Lee and his folks."

My eyes popped open, and I stared at Lee.

"His pa died, in the mine," Lee explained

My eyes and mouth opened wide with shock. I'd forgotten our fathers had worked in the same mine. It could just as easy have been Pa. "That's *terrible*. What *happened?*"

Lee's eyebrows rose. "You didn't hear? It was on the news for days. Gas exploded, the lower tunnels collapsed, and twelve men died."

I turned to Ricky, and his face froze flat with grief.

"I'm *so sorry.*" I didn't know what else to say and glanced up at Jake.

He spoke to Ricky in his low soft rumble. "How's your family doing?"

Ricky eyed Jake, cautiously assessing the large, bearded man. "Ma went to Kentucky, to her folks."

Jake raised an eyebrow. "You wanted to stay here?"

Ricky dropped his head and shrugged, digging his toe into the gravel. "There's not enough room there."

"You get to visit?"

"When school's done." Ricky raised his head and glared at Jake, desperation flooding his brown eyes. I understood; I'd felt that way before. Jake met those eyes with his gentle look and waited.

Lee shot me a glance, and I immediately responded. "Jake McDowell," I said, pointing at Jake. "Lee and Ricky." I waved at my friends.

Jake smiled and reached out a giant hand. Ricky grabbed it and hung on. When he let go, his eyes grew teary.

Lee and Jake shook hands, and I turned to Ricky. "Thanks for watchin' out for Lee."

He glanced up, surprised. "Guess I owed 'im that."

Lee grinned at me. "He's kinda like a brother, now. We fight, but more with words."

"It's nice of your folks to take him in," Jake said.

Lee eyed Jake and raised an eyebrow at me. I hurried to explain. "Jake and I met the first time I ran away. There was a hailstorm, and he let me take shelter. Then we got to talkin'…"

Lee took his time reading my face. When he turned to Jake, his dark eyes were very serious. "Thank you."

Jake's eyes widened with surprise, but it was typical for Lee, always two steps ahead of everybody else. Then Jake winked at Lee and glanced toward me with a smile. "He's worth the effort."

Lee snorted and Jake grinned as if they'd shared a private joke.

Ricky and I exchanged puzzled glances, but that made Lee laugh so hard he came near to falling.

Jake chuckled. "I like both your friends. Thanks for introducing us."

Then Lee and Ricky caught me up on all the news from school. We talked for over an hour before Jake nodded at the sun. It was time to go. I faked a punch at Lee and grabbed his shoulder as he punched and grabbed mine. I shook Ricky's hand, and they both shook Jake's hand before we left.

We hiked back slowly, almost in time for supper. Sarah, Pa, and Mamaw looked up from their meal when we walked in. Pa raised an eyebrow at Jake, who gave him a quick nod. I couldn't keep from staring at my pa. When I thought about the mine and imagined how he might have died, I came pretty close to tears. I bit my lip and glanced across the table at Jake. He made the slightest headshake. At first that puzzled me, and then I understood—he planned to tell Pa after supper.

Over the next weekend, Pa, Jake, and Mamaw spent a lot of time with Ma. I didn't have much homework and decided it was time to listen in. Saturday evening, while everyone but Ma was downstairs in the parlor, I tested all the walls next to her room and discovered I could hear best from inside Sarah's closet. The next morning, after church, I hid in there.

While I waited, I checked out Sarah's stuff. I couldn't believe she had so many clothes, and the top shelf of her closet overflowed with stuffed animals and dolls. Then I heard two sets of footsteps going up the stairs, sounding a lot like Pa and Jake. I put my ear to the wall, used my left ear without thinking, and realized that I favored that ear nowadays. Just never thought about it.

Ma started out complaining, mostly about Pa. Then Pa spoke up. "Are you sorry you married me? I know I ain't got no education. But I thought we were happy, up 'til you went to Memphis."

"Why do you always bring that up? You know what happened!" Ma's voice squeaked like a cornered animal, frightened and ready to strike back.

"I know 'bout Pete," Pa said. "I wanna know more 'bout you."

"Now you ask. For over a year you took me for a tramp. You treated me like dirt, went to work up in Kentucky, and even after I gave birth, you never said a word, never offered to hold me. What kind of marriage was that?"

"You coulda told me the truth." I heard Pa's anger and prayed he wouldn't start a fight.

"You know perfectly well why I didn't tell you."

There was silence. Pa finally spoke, his voice ragged, close to that dangerous breaking point. "You got no reason to be scairt. I've never hurt you."

"But I never know what will set you off. Everybody walks on eggshells when you're here, tolerating all your petty outbursts.

Our family lives in terror. And after what you did to Pete, I can't even trust you with the *kids*."

Somebody sobbed, and it shocked me to realize it was Pa.

Jake spoke, his low voice very gentle. "Can you tell us?" Then I heard Pa's footsteps running down the stairs. The front door slammed so hard the windows rattled.

Jake's footsteps didn't follow. "Do you know what happened?" he asked Ma.

"Some things, probably not the worst, and I can't say, not without his permission."

"I understand. Can you tell me if he ever has bad nightmares?"

Ma snorted. "*Terrible!* When he first got home, he really couldn't sleep. He'd wake up in a cold sweat, shaking and screaming. He acted so confused, he frightened me. Now that he's strong again, he works himself so hard he passes out, and then he only sleeps about four hours. He's lived that way for years. But with this security guard job, that can't happen. And now I'm really scared—for him and for everybody else."

I wished I could see right through the wall. I knew Jake would nod, or raise his eyebrows, or something.

At last he spoke. "Does he stare into space or do anything scary?"

Ma's response could've been a headshake or a nod. This was worse than *not* listening, and I wanted to help Pa. I left Sarah's closet and tiptoed down the stairs. But when I looked outside, his car was gone.

Pa didn't return until very late that night, and I kept waking 'til I heard him on the stairs. At dawn the next morning, he knocked on my door, bugging me about the FBI. He looked like shit, half-shaved, his eyes bloodshot with dark bags underneath. I felt so sorry for him that I finally agreed to see their pictures. He made an appointment the same day and called in *sick*. In my entire life, I'd never known him to call in sick.

While we drove into Knoxville, I imagined the FBI worked someplace new and fancy, like one of those big buildings in Washington, DC. But we parked in front of an old office building, and the agent who met us was a lady. She looked the same age as Ma but not as pretty, with straight brown hair pulled back so tight her eyes bulged. When she led us to a room and brought out a book of pictures, she squinted her bug eyes at me and said, "Look carefully at each one and tell me if you've seen him."

So I did. I wasn't near as scared as I expected, probably 'cause none of the pictures looked familiar. Then she brought out another book. This went on for hours, and I got totally fed up. Pa stayed so nervous he jiggled his feet. That didn't help my mood a bit.

With her bug eyes narrowed in frustration, the lady agent asked, "Can you describe them?"

My stomach lurched like I was falling. I glanced at Pa, but he stayed silent.

"Maybe one or two, I couldn't really look." My mind flashed to the gun against my throat. For the first time that day, I felt real shaky.

She brought another person into the room, an artist, and he asked me to describe one of the men. I tried to picture the leader, mostly because Pa hated him the most. But I couldn't find words to describe his type of face, much less the exact shape of his nose, mouth, and ears, or the color of his eyes. I was so lousy at describing, they both left.

"Sorry," I told Pa.

"At least you tried."

He kept on fidgeting, his voice stretched tight, and I knew he hadn't slept at all. Since I agreed to come here, I wanted to do something that would help both him and Ma. I thought long and hard about the man they left to guard me, the man who got mad and shot his gun next to my ear. His face stood out in my mind in so much detail even I could draw it. I grabbed a sheet of paper and a pencil and drew.

Pa watched, his eyes and mouth wide open. "Hey, that's pretty good—that one of them?"

I nodded.

"Which one?"

"The one guarding me."

Pa jumped up and took my picture to the agent. She came back and asked me to draw another man. I drew the leader, the guy next to him, and the two who held Ma down. I wasn't scared at all, and that surprised me. I'd forgotten how much I liked to draw.

"Can you tell me about them?" the lady agent asked. But soon as she spoke, my mind erased the memory like an eraser on a chalkboard. I stared at her, frozen in my seat.

Pa turned to me. "Which one is the leader?"

I pointed.

"Which one held you at gunpoint?"

I pointed to the first picture I drew. One by one, he got me to identify them all. Then he went with the agent and gave her the whole story, or at least the parts he knew.

On the way home, I started feeling sick. Pa stopped and bought us each a soda. While I sipped mine, he asked, "Where'd you learn to draw?"

I nearly panicked. If I told him the truth, it'd make him angry, and he was already stretched too thin. But I'd been trying not to lie, and he'd been trying to be good…

I tossed the dice. "I drew at school. I took my comic books and copied all the pictures. I even made up stories and drew all the scenes. Then Miss Clausen got so mad, she cleaned out my desk and threw everythin' I drew into the trash."

Pa didn't say a word, and as soon as we got home, he went outside and dug up the garden for spring planting. But at supper that night, he bragged on me. He told the whole family how I drew all the pictures, said I drew better pictures than the FBI's artist. From across the table, Jake caught my eye and winked, and I knew for sure I'd done all right.

Chapter 20

Later that week, Mamaw took me to the doctor. He peered into my ears and then agreed with Jake. My right eardrum was busted and I needed surgery.

Mamaw made an appointment with a surgeon in Oak Ridge. It wasn't far away, but I'd never been there. Pa said it'd been a secret military base during the war, and their scientists designed the first atom bomb. Everybody else said the place was radioactive. Pa pooh-poohed that. He said they locked up all the radioactive stuff and kept it guarded day and night. I imagined the city as a giant fort with a monstrous underground vault.

When we actually drove into Oak Ridge, I stared all around me in surprise. Once you passed the guard gates, the city looked like any other town. The hospital seemed newer and nicer than Harriman's, and in the surgeon's office, plaques covered the wall. Mamaw said they were awards and diplomas from his college. I figured if it took that many years to go to school, I would never be a doctor.

After a long wait, the surgeon joined us. He looked in both my ears, did a hearing test, and eventually he, too, agreed with Jake. Then he sent me for x-rays of my head, and once those were developed, he compared my pictures to his model of an ear. It was cool. He explained how the ear worked and why mine didn't work with a broke eardrum. Mamaw scheduled my surgery for the first Wednesday in March.

At home, Mamaw pushed me to finish up my schoolwork, and then she announced that I'd completed the fifth grade. That made me feel good, but she didn't let me stop. She hurried out to buy me sixth-grade books.

Over the next month, Jake's cough improved, although it never disappeared. But he acted normal, more like last summer. Early each morning, he took off for the creek and brought home catfish for the freezer. After dinner he helped Mamaw with her chores and sometimes made repairs around the house. And after school, he talked and fished with me, even showed me how to tune up Mamaw's car. That pleased Pa 'cause he didn't have the time.

Jake spent an hour with Ma most every day. I eavesdropped from time to time. Sometimes they talked about that ugly night in Memphis, sometimes they talked about Pa, and sometimes they chatted like old friends. He never got angry, even when she launched her mean attacks. Recently I noticed he was smiling when he left, so I planned to listen in again.

One early afternoon, before Sarah got home, I snuck into her closet and heard Jake asking questions. I could picture his face—real serious—while he listened carefully to Ma.

"What happens in your head when you see Pete?"

"I get upset. I want him to leave, leave me alone. I can't stand to see him, and I'm sure he hates me, for everything he's been through and everything I've said. I don't even know where to begin."

"Upset? Like scared or angry or confused?"

"Like I want to run away, but I can't."

"Are there other times you feel like running?"

"When I think about the rape. I wanted to run then, but they held me. And no matter how hard I fought, they could hold me down and make me do anything they wanted. It was *terrible.* I never want to be that helpless again—*ever!"*

Ma cried softly, which always made me sad. Even when she hated me and told me ugly things, I didn't want to make her cry.

"It's a scary feeling, being helpless." Jake spoke in his soothing rumble. "Do you feel helpless when Pete walks in the room?"

Ma stayed silent for a minute before speaking. "No, I have control. I escape by getting rid of him."

"Once he leaves, do you feel any better?"

"I feel terrible, like a *monster."* Ma cried again.

Jake waited, letting her calm down before he spoke. "What would happen if you didn't make him leave?"

"I'm not sure." Ma paused and sniffed. "If he doesn't leave, I turn away, make believe he's gone. But if I pay attention—to *him*? I don't think I can; I get too mad."

"Let's try a different kind of make-believe," Jake said. From his voice, I knew he was smiling. "Let's make believe that Pete is in the room, right over here." He tapped the wall next to my ear. "I want you to picture him there and talk to him."

My eyes popped wide, and I almost ran away. Did Jake actually know where I sat listening? But my curiosity held me prisoner. What would she say?

"Hi, Pete." Her voice trembled. "I still want him gone," she told Jake.

"That's okay, keep talking."

"How's school? Do you need any new clothes or a haircut?" Her voice grew stronger, but then she said to Jake. "I have no idea what he wants. He's growing up and changing so fast, I hardly know him."

"I think you're doing great." Jake's voice soothed her. "You just need practice. Practice thinking about Pete and picturing his face, until you work out exactly what you want to say. You'll be glad you practiced when you're faced with the real thing!"

"You think he'll ever forgive me?" Ma sounded sad.

"I think he'll be fine, unless you trigger him. Like you, he has bad dreams and reminders set him off, but I don't think he sees you as a trigger. He does talk about a bad man in his head, a voice that tells him to act out. So at first, you might want to stick to neutral topics."

"That's *terrible*." Ma said. "He's much too young to have experience with such things."

"He'll be okay. Pete's a very resilient young man."

I wondered what "resilient" meant and made a mental note to ask Mamaw. It was past time for Sarah to get home, so I snuck back into my room as if I'd never left it. But when Jake left Ma's bedroom and headed for the stairs, he saw me on my bed and gave a wink. I swear he knew.

On the morning of my surgery, Mamaw said I couldn't eat, and for once in my life I didn't feel the least bit hungry—my stomach stayed tied up in knots. Pa drove me and Mamaw to Oak Ridge. Sarah went to school, and Jake stayed behind with Ma.

The nurses dressed me in a gown. If I hadn't been so nervous, I would have objected. Then they stuck a huge needle in my arm, attached me to a pole, and rolled me into a big, high-ceilinged room with blinding lights.

When they placed a mask against my face, the doctor said, "Breathe deep." After that, I didn't remember anything at all until the nurse told me to wake up.

Mamaw's voice echoed in my head. "You did great. Everything went well, and the doctor tells me you can hear."

I opened my eyes and saw her, leaning over my right ear. A grin slowly spread across my face.

When Pa picked me up the next morning, he seemed in an unusually good mood. "I got a big surprise for you," he said, and he kept me guessing all the way back home. Soon as I got there, I rushed up the steps and through the door.

Ma was sitting in the parlor. I almost turned around and walked back out. Pa put his arm around my shoulders and stopped me.

"Hi, Pete," Ma said.

For no reason at all, my eyes grew teary.

"How's the ear?"

"Okay. I can hear now."

"That's great!" Ma smiled. She looked real pretty when she smiled. "Mamaw told me you finished the fifth grade."

"Yeah, I guess. She bought me sixth-grade books."

Ma's face tensed, and I started to get worried, but she pulled herself together. "I wanted to thank you for going to the FBI and drawing all those pictures. I'm so relieved— all those terrible men are in *jail*."

Shocked by her words, I completely forgot about Jake's warning. "They arrested the men? Will I have to testify?"

"Yes, they've been arrested. And no, you won't testify. Your pa and I agree that you already did your part. And it's also more effective if I go."

Ma stayed calm, and her courage amazed me. Was everybody in my family brave except for me?

We'd run out of things to say, and silence made me nervous. I kept expecting her to tell me I should die. Instead she said, "I have to help with supper," and disappeared through the kitchen door.

I stared after her and then at Pa. Could I be dreaming? Maybe half-asleep, still in recovery?

"She's okay?"

He grinned. "She's been better ever since they caught the gang. The lady agent said they been tailin' those men for several months, but they didn't have the evidence to hold 'em. You gave 'em exactly what they needed."

I stood there, stunned. All I'd done was draw some pictures. "Where's Jake?"

"He's cleanin' out his shed, and I'm 'bout to pick him up. Wanna come?

Pa and I drove to Harriman. As I trotted down the hill, I saw Jake stuffing his old junk into paper garbage bags. He'd made a smaller pile of things he planned to keep. Small enough, I guessed, for him to carry.

"Hi guys!" he yelled when he saw us. "I'm almost finished. Pete, this is yours." He handed me the bamboo fishing pole he'd made last year.

"Thanks!"

"How's the ear?"

"Great. I can hear again." I grinned.

Jake smiled back. He didn't seem surprised, so Mamaw must have told him.

"Help Jake take his stuff up to the car," Pa said.

I gathered the sleeping bag and blankets under one arm and grabbed the fishing pole with my other hand. Jake took all the rest, and we climbed up the hill to our car.

I turned around so Jake could hear. "Ma told me they arrested the bad men."

Jake stepped up beside me. "Yeah, I know. How do you feel about it?"

"Okay, I guess. Ma said I don't have to testify. *She* plans to go and talk in court."

Jake nodded, obviously a part of that decision.

"You movin' out?" I asked.

"I'll be staying at your place until June, but the owner wants the shed emptied since I'm gone."

"Just 'til June? Where will you go?"

"We'll see."

Jake hadn't really answered, and that created a new worry. But I felt so jazzed about talking with Ma and catching all the bad guys, I couldn't take the time for it right then.

That night, Ma helped Mamaw serve us supper. As soon as Ma sat down at her end of the table, the entire room seemed more in balance, like we'd been living on a tilting teeter-totter and Ma's presence held it level. Or maybe our home had been designed around her, and her absence made an empty place that no one else could fill. Either way, I relaxed. The corners of my mouth started curving upward, and I saw that same smile on Sarah and Pa's faces. Jake met my eyes and grinned. All was well.

Mamaw left in May. By that time, Ma could handle all the housework and the cooking. It made me sad, seeing Mamaw go, and I thanked her for teaching me all year. But I understood—she needed a vacation, and she wanted to spend time with Aunt Kate.

As June approached, I began worrying about Jake. Then one day I saw him packing up his room, and I asked him again, "Where you goin'?"

"Well, first I plan to visit my sister in Alaska—haven't been to see her in years. But before winter comes, I'll hop a freighter, probably for New Zealand or Australia. I made myself a promise to spend my fifty-first birthday in the sun."

I stared in disbelief. "You're really leavin'!"

"I'm a wanderer, Pete." Jake smiled, though the corners of his eyes drooped. "But before I go anywhere, I really need to thank you. I'd almost given up when you and your pa came, but with Mamaw's pills and food, my health is much improved. And talking with all of you taught me things as well. Since prison I'd been terrified to live near other folks, but I did okay here. I think you and your family helped me more than I helped you."

That should have made me happy and proud, but it didn't. On the verge of tears, I said, "Will you come back?"

"Of course." His drooping eyes sought mine. "I plan to be here next year for your twelfth birthday."

"A whole *year?*" Tears flooded my eyes, and I fought hard to stop them.

"A year only seems long when you're ten. In a few more days, you'll be eleven, and time will go by much faster. I'll send you lots of postcards, so you'll always know where I am."

I still didn't like it. "What if you get sick—or die?"

Jake lowered his eyes to the floor and sighed. His expression turned serious as he looked up at me. "Death isn't permanent, Pete. It's just a door into a different way of being. If I die, my spirit will find you. Any time you need me, I'll be there."

Jake reached under his bed and pulled out a small package. "It's your birthday present, but you can open it today."

I broke the string and tore off the brown paper. Inside I found a heavy, folded map. As I opened it, Jake said, "Let's hang it in your room, over your bed. That way you can always see exactly where I am."

The map, printed on thick, glossy paper, showed every country in the entire world. It looked real impressive on my wall. That made me realize how bare my room had been ever since I tore down Superman.

"Thanks." I hugged him, my head against his chest. He held me tight.

Saying goodbye to Jake threw me back in time, into the terrible year before we ever met. I felt as if a dark cloud stayed right in front of me, blocking all the sunshine from my life. Pa asked me what I wanted for my birthday, and I told him I wanted to go fly-fishing with Jake. He agreed that sounded like good fun. Then Ma and Sarah said they'd bring us lunch, so they'd come too. I wanted to enjoy the fishing trip but knew I wouldn't.

The day before my birthday, Pa washed and polished his new car, a '55 Ford Fairlane, bright red with a white stripe on both sides. He'd bought it with the money he got from the Feds. Together, he, Jake, and I loaded all the rods and bait and tackle boxes into the trunk and backseat. Pa planned for us to leave at dawn.

I couldn't sleep. Even the soft rattle of Jake's snoring in the attic just reminded me that he'd be gone. What if something awful happened and I couldn't find him? Who would I talk to? What if I had nightmares? I gave up on sleep and went downstairs.

"Hi, Pete."

In the darkness, Ma's voice startled me. I flipped on the hall light, which reflected off her golden hair. Sitting at the kitchen table, dressed in a long white robe, she looked like an angel, or maybe an evil witch disguised. Uncertain, I turned away and made myself some toast.

"Are you excited about your birthday trip tomorrow?"

"Not really. I'm worryin' 'bout Jake."

"Of course. He's leaving soon."

"Monday, for Alaska. But then he's gonna travel to Australia or New Zealand. I won't see him for a *year*."

"I know you'll miss him, but you have to let people be themselves. He's always been a wanderer—he loves it. You wouldn't want to stop him from doing what he loves?"

I dropped my toast on a plate and sat across from her, searching her face. "Like you love singin'?"

"Yes, I suppose it's much the same."

"Do you ever plan to sing again?"

Ma reached over, opened the cupboard, and handed me a jar of peanut butter. I spread it on my toast and munched slowly, wondering if she would even answer.

"Not right now," she finally said. "Right now I want to stay with you and Sarah. It won't be that long before you both move out. And then I might."

"You don't think Jake is happy living here?"

Ma was quiet for a while before speaking. "Jake doesn't have a family, and I know that seeing ours is difficult for him— reminds him every day of what he lost. But he enjoys helping people, and traveling lets him meet all kinds of folks. You can't change him, Pete, but I really think he loves you. He'll be back."

And just like that, I felt better. Ma and I could talk about a problem, and some things I could talk about with Pa or even Sarah. And now that school was out, I could meet with Lee and Ricky. I couldn't wait to see them both again.

"Thanks!" I finished my toast. Then I climbed the stairs, curled up in my bed, and fell into a deep, dreamless sleep.

Chapter 21

The morning of my eleventh birthday, a light fog layer hid the sky. The early glow of dawn bathed the sleeping countryside in a mysterious, smoky green. A color, Jake assured me, only found in Tennessee.

We three guys took off in our new car, Pa driving. Since it was my birthday, Jake insisted I ride shotgun while he lounged in the back. We drove north into the Cumberlands and turned off at a state park, following that road to its end. We parked where the ladies planned to meet us later on, grabbed our gear, and took off up the trail.

The grass grew thick and deep, and in places the overgrown bushes hid the path but Pa led the way without any hesitation. Suddenly the thicket opened into a lush meadow with mountains in the background and a deep fast-flowing stream.

"Wow!" Jake exclaimed. "Wish I'd found this place a few years back."

"Family secret," Pa said with a smile.

While I tied a fly onto my hook, Jake grabbed one of Pa's poles and began to rearrange it, adding more line to the end with hook and fly.

Pa watched as he worked. "You gotta teach me that."

"It's easy. Fly-fishing is just an old-fashioned way to fish. It's not all that efficient, but it's fun. Here, I'll show you." Jake demonstrated how he cast the fly and made it dance like a real fly skimming on the water. I watched and wished I could do it like he did.

Then Pa tried while Jake coached him. I grabbed my bamboo pole and wandered upstream. I tested the water—cool but not too cold—took off my shoes, and waded in.

Upstream, I found the perfect spot, a little overhang where the early morning sun dappled the still water. I cast out and played the line.

He struck—the biggest trout I'd ever seen! I set the hook, and he jumped straight up out of the stream. Then he dove and took off running. I splashed into deeper water and followed him as far as I could go. When I jerked the line, he jumped again.

Pa and Jake heard the splash and walked closer to watch. I paid them no mind, completely focused on the fish, anticipating every leap and dive. We played cat-and- mouse until I was plumb tuckered, but so was the fish. As I pulled the line in, he surfaced one last time, and Jake snagged him in the net.

"Damn big fish." Pa nearly knocked me over with a slap on my back.

Jake lifted the trout up by its gills and said, "Wish I had a camera—this one's a beauty."

None of us thought to check the sky, and right at that moment, the heavens burst loose with a torrential rainfall that threatened to flood us out. I still had my fishing pole, Pa ran to rescue his, and Jake followed, carrying my fish. By then we were as soaked as if we'd been swimming in a lake.

Jake laughed, a deep belly laugh. Pa and I started laughing too, and soon we were howling like three drunken lunatics. Maybe we were crazy, but it sure felt good. We ignored the rain and took our time gathering and repacking all our gear. We hiked back down the mountain through the downpour. About the time we reached the car, the rain eased off a bit. We loaded up our stuff and stripped off our drenched clothes down to our shorts.

Pa and Jake were joking with each other while I gathered up the buckets we'd brought to carry fish. They'd filled with rain, so I grabbed one and sloshed most of it on Jake. He laughed, reached for the other one, and threw that bucketful on me. While dodging him, I threw the rest at Pa.

Pa roared like I'd scalded him, his face a death mask as he lunged after me. I scrambled to escape, and Jake stepped between us. Pa nearly slammed into Jake's body. He stopped just in time, fists clenched and eyes glaring.

"Whoa there, Rob," Jake said. "What's wrong?"

Pa's expression shifted to confusion.

Jake's voice softened to a soothing rumble. "You okay?"

Pa barely shook his head. Jake returned his puzzled gaze with understanding. "Want to sit in the car and dry off?" He opened the passenger-side door; Pa climbed inside. Jake motioned to me, and we walked around to the driver's side. I slid in behind him, as far from Pa as I could get.

Jake found the keys and turned on the fan. I handed Pa a towel from the floor. He still looked confused, but when he dried his face, it seemed to help.

"Want to talk about it?" Jake asked.

Pa glanced back at me.

"I think Pete should be included."

Pa hesitated, but then he turned around, facing me. His voice cracked as he told me, "I got caught...by the Japs."

"You were a POW?" That was the last thing I would have guessed.

"Yeah."

"Does Ma know?"

"Of course. It's no secret, but it's nothin' I'm proud of."

"How'd they catch you?" I asked.

"I was shot...in the leg."

Jake watched Pa closely, eyes narrowed in concern. "Where were you?"

Pa snorted. "Some tiny island out in the Pacific, not even worth the trouble, 'cept the Japs built an airport in the center. They'd been shootin' at our bombers, and we went in to find the guns."

"What happened next?" I asked.

"A sniper got me. Our medic stopped the bleedin', and our lieutenant decided to go on. He told me to hide 'til they got back." Pa took a couple deep breaths before continuing. "Soon as they left, a dozen Japs dropped from the trees. They disarmed me and dragged me to the airport. When their translator came, he promised to fix my leg if I told 'em what I knew."

"What'd you do?" I asked.

"I told 'em we were lookin' for fresh water, had a problem with the water on the ship."

"Did they believe that?" Jake asked.

Pa shrugged. "They removed the bullet, even gave me penicillin."

"Were you there when our bombers came?"

"No. Weather closed in, and soon as it cleared, the Japs put me on ship to Malaysia. I stayed on the island for a couple weeks and on the ship for a couple more. My leg had mostly healed when we docked."

"And the camp?"

Pa sighed and looked down at the car floor. "Disgustin'. No real sanitation, no real barracks, just thatched huts that leaked— and it rained 'most every day. We got one meal a day, and most of the men had some kinda dysentery."

I didn't understand everything he said, but from Jake's expression, it was nasty. "What'd you do there?" I asked.

Pa grimaced. "Slave labor—built roads and bridges, repaired anythin' the Allies bombed."

"How long were you there?"

"Almost a year."

Jake and I waited as Pa stayed silent, staring off into space. After some time, he hung his head and took a long, deep breath. He rubbed his forehead with both hands and began.

"I got to know our medic, Aussie kid named Sam. Since the guards stole most of our medical supplies, he had to beg for what we needed."

Pa hid his face, but I knew he was upset. I watched his hands became fists and his arm muscles bulge. He breathed hard, like he'd been running.

"We all got sick—dysentery, fevers. Men keeled over in the heat. Sam did a lotta beggin'. This one guard, a high rankin' Jap, *hated* Sam.*"*

Pa's voice grew dangerously high, and he lifted a face twisted with rage. I knew that face. Shuddering, I huddled near the door.

"If Sam asked for anythin', that bastard beat 'im—broke his nose, blacked his eyes, knocked out teeth. Made me *furious*. One day he 'most killed Sam…but I stopped him."

Pa's hands began to shake. Jake had stayed quiet, allowing Pa to talk. But when Pa started trembling, Jake said, "Rob, it's okay. You're safe."

Pa bellowed and nearly pulled the handle off the car door. I'd seen Jake lock the doors earlier, though I didn't realize I'd be stuck inside with Pa. I wanted to run almost as bad as he did. Jake didn't flinch; he just continued talking real quiet.

Pa's eyes glazed over with a wild, crazy stare, his lips pulled back into an agonized grimace. His breathing rasped in short, gasping breaths. Jake's forehead furrowed, his eyes riveted on Pa's distorted face. Then he did exactly what he'd told me *not* to do. He touched Pa's arm lightly with his fingers.

"*You bastard!*" Pa turned on Jake, hands grasping for his throat.

Jake shoved Pa back against the door, keeping his own neck out of reach. "*Rob*, you're stateside with me and Pete," he said in a clear, firm voice. "You're safe. You're home."

Pa's eyes flickered, and Jake kept talking. "You're in Tennessee, with Pete, you're okay."

Pa dropped his hands, and Jake released his hold. After several minutes, Pa croaked, "Sorry."

"No harm done," Jake said. "Can you tell me what they did?"

Pa cast a desperate glance at Jake, who returned a gentle, steady gaze.

"It's okay, Rob. I know you're hurting. But if you can talk about it, that will make it better." Jake extended both his hands, palms up. "You don't have to relive it. Try watching your memory from a distance, like a movie. And if you'll take my hands, I'll squeeze to remind you that you're safe."

Pa hesitated but then took a firm hold on Jake's hands. When he spoke, his breathing came in gasps. "They used clubs...broke my nose...got me on the ground ...broke ribs... near to *killed* me...stuffed me in a cage, all bent over...hurt to breathe.

Pa panted, mouth open, face pulled tight, and he gripped Jake's hands so hard I feared he'd break them.

"You're okay, Rob," Jake whispered. "Stay with me."

"Couldn't sleep. I'd nod off...they poured water...*choked me*..." Pa's whole body jerked.

Jake squeezed Pa's hands even tighter and commanded, "Look at me!" Pa obeyed and recognition flickered in his eyes. His shoulders sagged.

"You're with us. You're okay," Jake repeated, his voice calm, his eyes holding steady on Pa's stare.

Pa kept his eyes on Jake, but his voice rose high and tight. "By the third day, I was crazy…constant pain…no sleep…sure I'd die…that devil dragged Sam where I could see …beat him… tortured him…to death!"

The dead piano player flashed before my eyes. Jake glanced at me, eyebrows raised. But I hadn't lost it, not completely, so he turned to Pa and asked, "What were you thinking as you watched?"

"I killed Sam!"

Jake stayed quiet, and Pa rested several minutes 'til his breathing slowed to normal. Eyes bloodshot, face streaked with tears, he let go of Jake and turned to me. When he spoke, his voice sounded almost steady.

"Your school called and told me what you'd done, and I thought, *that Jap devil!* That's why I lost it, Pete. I'm so sorry. I never wanted to hurt *you!*"

He reached out, and I jumped back. Behind Pa, Jake shook his head. Hands trembling, I leaned forward and lightly touched Pa's shoulders. Pa didn't attack; he looked close to crying.

I whispered in his ear, "I love you, Pa."

He broke down sobbing, and I put both arms around his shoulders, squeezing tight. From the corner of my eye, I saw Jake relax.

When Pa finished crying, I scooted back and curled up in my seat, completely drained. Jake spoke in a very quiet voice. "I swear, Rob, I don't know how you survived. And more than survived—you've led a pretty normal life. How did you manage?"

Pa wiped his face with the towel. "It was Helga. I kept thinkin' 'bout her. After a week, they dragged me from that cage and ordered me right back to slave labor. Another prisoner taped my nose and ribs. But I was weak, and some days I hurt so bad, I prayed the guards would kill me." Pa's breathing raced again, and he stopped talking 'til it slowed. "Then I'd think of Helga and keep movin'."

Pa hunched over in his seat. For several minutes he looked too exhausted to sit up or even lift his head. When he spoke, he barely whispered.

"We ran out of food near the end, and when our troops arrived I couldn't even stand, but I kept dreamin' 'bout Helga. On the ship home, they fed us well, and by the time we reached Hawaii, I could walk. Helga ran over, threw her arms around me, and bawled. Then she helped in every way she knew." Pa's eyes leaked tears as he remembered.

"Like you helped her," Jake said, his own eyes overflowing. He bit hard on his lip, and I knew he had to be thinking about Matilda. I feared *he'd* lose it, and for several minutes he fought hard to keep control. Finally he sighed deep and turned to Pa. "You know, that Jap guard would have killed Sam anyway."

Pa leaned back against the seat, eyes closed, and nodded. "I figured that part out. He did the killin', not me." He snorted. "I was stupid. Shoulda realized I warn't no Superman."

Jake shrugged. "In a different setting, you'd have been a hero. In the camps, that was close to suicide. You get any therapy after you got back?"

Pa's eyes flew open and he scowled. "That psycho shit?"

Jake raised his eyebrows. "What happened?"

Pa clenched his fists and sat up straight. "There in Nashville, I tried to tell 'em what I just told you and lost control—kinda like today. But *they* tied me to a cot and left me helpless. I really believed I was back there...in that cage." Pa started panting, eyes wide. Jake reached out his hands, and Pa held on.

After he calmed down, Pa closed his eyes and leaned back again, looking exhausted but relaxed. Jake started coughing and turned his head away. I finally understood why Pa acted so crazy at the VA hospital. The place triggered him, made him relive all that pain, and he never would have gone there except to rescue me. I bit my lip hard to keep from crying.

Jake stopped coughing, but his face and posture remained tense. He quietly admitted, "This is one of those times I could really use a drink."

"Me too," Pa sighed. "But that ain't happenin'."

"You know what I miss most when I'm sober?" Jake rubbed his hands, which still showed imprints from Pa's nails digging in.

"What?" Pa half-opened his eyes and studied Jake.

"The barroom camaraderie, the laughter, and the songs. I really liked it."

That brought the flicker of a smile to Pa's face. "You know any good songs?"

"They're not *good*." Jake raised an eyebrow and glanced back at me.

Pa shrugged. "He's seen and heard a lot worse."

Jake rumbled out a verse of "Waltzing Matilda" that I'd never heard anywhere before. Pa smiled and came up with another filthy verse. They traded memories and verses while I listened and joined in. They were treating me just like a man!

By late morning, the rain still hadn't stopped. Jake drove us home, and Ma met us at the door. She took a long hard look at Pa and squeezed his hands. He put his arms around her and buried his face in her blond hair.

Jake helped me clean the trout, and Sarah fried it. Then we held my birthday picnic in the kitchen. Ma had even baked a cake. That meant I could make a wish and blow out all the candles.

I wanted to wish that things would never change, that our family would always be together. But Jake said change was the one thing you could count on, and our lives were already changing. Some for the better—Ma for certain—and some for the worse. I would certainly miss Jake. And there might be changes we couldn't even guess. I gave control over to Lord Jesus, and instead of wishing, I said a little prayer.

"Dear Lord Jesus, please help us tell the truth, 'specially the ugly truths that we want to hide. And protect us from evil, 'specially the evil that lives inside each one of us. And may your will be done, here on earth and in heaven, Amen."

On Sunday Jake joined us at our church. Afterwards he walked to the creek with Ma and Pa. I figured Pa would tell Ma everything he told me—with Jake's help. When they got back, Ma started fixing supper, and Jake went upstairs to pack. But Pa looked so hangdog, I thought he might start crying.

"What's wrong?" I asked.

Pa headed for the sofa in the parlor. We sat down. "I asked Jake to stay, be a part of our family." Pa's voice croaked. "He said he cain't."

"Did he say why?"

Pa stared at the floor. "He said a lotta things, but none of it made any sense to me."

I could tell Pa was struggling with letting go of Jake the same as I'd struggled a couple days before. I decided to tell him what helped me.

"Ma said it hurts Jake, seein' our family—probably 'cause he lost his own. He cried yesterday when you were talkin' about Ma, and I'm pretty sure my visit made him drink. But he loves to travel, to meet and help new people, and he promised to come back."

Pa's face grew thoughtful. Then he reached over and gave me a big hug. That was my best birthday present—ever.

Chapter 22

Jake sent me a card when he reached Fairbanks, and I put a red dot on my map, the one he'd given me for my birthday. After that I didn't hear anything for months.

Christmas had passed before I got a letter. The postmark read Alaska, but the handwriting looked different. I started worrying before I even tore it open. A small blue book and note fell on my bed. I read the note.

Dear Pete,

Jake wanted you to have this. You can withdraw it once you turn eighteen. Please keep it safe until then. He thought the world of you and your folks and repeatedly told me how you took him in your home and treated him like a member of your family.

I'm very sorry to have to tell you this, but Jake didn't make it to Australia. He said he never told you, but over a year ago, the VA found a spot on his right lung. Jake didn't follow up, and when he started feeling better, he decided it was nothing. But after he'd been here a while, he got worse. By the time he saw a doctor, there was nothing they could do.

186

Early in December, Jake flew to an Inuit village near the coast. We lived close by when he was just a boy. It's where he learned to hunt and fish. They have a tradition of walking on the ice, a sacred path for folks about to die. Jake chose to honor that tradition.

The fishermen told me Jake walked a long ways out, almost to the edge where the ice meets the sea. Then he sat down, drank a bottle of Scotch, and went to sleep one last time. That night a blizzard came and buried him, and this spring the ocean he so dearly loved will become his final resting place.

I know this is hard for you to read. But please remember he enjoyed those months with you more than anything he'd done since the War. Thank you for your kindness, and remember that he loved you very much.

Sincerely,

Catherine McDowell Fisher, Jake's sister

I sat frozen with shock as tears streamed down my cheeks. I wanted to scream, beat my head, and tear the letter into tiny, ugly pieces. But I knew that wouldn't change the truth.

Ma came in. I handed her the letter, and she got all teary eyed. Then she opened up the little book and gasped. "There's close to a thousand dollars, Pete—almost enough to pay for your college!"

I didn't care about the money. Jake and I had made so many plans. Every night as I stared at the map above my bed, I longed to be eighteen, old enough to work and travel. He'd talked about us going to see Paris, Rome, and London. We'd planned to sail to Egypt, travel down through Africa, and then visit Asia and Australia. I'd never be able to do that without Jake!

I spent the rest of the afternoon in such deep despair I couldn't talk. I didn't even eat. That evening I reached beneath my bed to find a book and pulled out a long forgotten *Superman* comic. I thought I'd burned them all. But this was the one I used to carry in my pocket, the one where Superman got trapped with Kryptonite and nearly died. I read it over and over 'til my eyes burned. Inside the cover, I found my little flag and placed it on the picture of Superman near dying, just to remind him help would come.

Jake had come and helped us, changed our lives. He shared his truth, even when it hurt him, and he listened closely as we struggled to tell ours. He helped us find the courage to keep living, even when he knew he might die.

I sobbed, but that seemed selfish. Every single day for the last dozen years, Jake had battled grief, addiction, waking dreams, and illness, and now he walked with Jesus and his long-lost wife and son. But I still wanted him with *me*! Breathing deep, I prayed, asking Lord Jesus to give my thanks to Jake. I felt real bad because I'd never said it. Praying helped, so I kept on praying until my mind settled down.

I felt Jake with me, and his gentle presence soothed away my tears. Suddenly unafraid, I smiled, almost laughed. Jake told me the truth, and this time I understood. First off, he reminded me that death is temporary. Second, that I'd never be alone, 'cause anytime I got into trouble, he'd be there. And the final truth, the most important one of all: his love would always live inside my heart—a kinder, stronger, braver part of me.